JAMES BLOND
STOCKPORT IS TOO MUCH

by

Terry Ravenscroft

Grosvenor House
Publishing Limited

This book is published by
Grosvenor House Publishing Ltd
28-30 High Street, Guildford, Surrey, GU1 3HY.
www.grosvenorhousepublishing.co.uk

A CIP record for this book
is available from the British Library

ISBN 978-1-908105-25-7

Cover artwork by Tony Colligan   www.tctoons.com

ABOUT THE AUTHOR

The day after Terry Ravenscroft threw in his mundane factory job to write television comedy scripts and books he was involved in a car accident which left him unable to turn his head. Since then he has never looked back. Born in New Mills, Derbyshire, in 1938, he still lives there with his wife Delma and his mistress Divine Bottom (in his dreams). His other books are Air Mail, Dear Customer Services, Football Crazy, Captain's Day & Inflatable Hugh. He has a website www.topcomedy.co.uk

CHAPTER ONE

NEVER SAY ALWAYS ON

James Blond, British Secret Service agent SA-Seven, slowly turned the door handle and gently eased open the door to the girl's apartment. His current assignment successfully completed, it was time for a little extra-curricular activity before returning to England and Paramount Holdings, the property development company based in London which covertly served as a front for MI6. If nothing else it would help to clear from his mind the unpleasant business he'd had to carry out earlier that evening. Killing someone never came easy to Blond, even though he had killed many times before; and even when the villain he had been ordered to dispatch was scum like Morientes, an evil parasite who made his living off the suffering of others.

The Mexican had been a drug baron and therefore in Blond's eyes the very lowest scum; the world would be a happier place without the drugs. True, it was also a happier place with them, much happier, especially if the drug in question was a few grams of top quality Colombian up your nose. However Blond, no stranger to the occasional line himself, knew as well as anyone that the effect of drugs was ephemeral, that the euphoria a drug brought with it would very quickly be surpassed many times over by the dark depression that inevitably followed.

And the drugs that Morientes dealt were not merely cocaine, a substance that could be kept under control. It was something harder and much more dangerous.

Heroin. The big H. Well now the Mexican was in the big H in the sky, if you believed in that sort of thing, or more probably the big H below, and good riddance to him.

He had first seen the girl in the cocktail bar of the Sandals in which he'd been staying. She had been in the company of a man, a suitor judging by the close attention he paid her. It hadn't stopped her returning Blond's smile on the couple of occasions he had managed to catch her eye, however. He had followed the couple at a safe distance when they left and had thanked his lucky stars when the man dropped her off at the apartment block. Now, some five minutes later, he was entering her apartment.

The girl was drop dead gorgeous. No other words to describe her. On seeing her again Blond, being Blond, immediately began to wonder what she would be like in bed. Passive? Active? A talker? A screamer? He had made love to them all, and many times over. Well it wouldn't be long before he found out; he was sure to bed the girl, it was a cast iron certainty, he always did.

Blond would have been lying if he had tried to claim he didn't enjoy the company of women. Yet he invariably treated them casually. Indeed there were some people who would claim, not without some justification, that he treated women as nothing more nor less than a sort of de-luxe willy warmer. But they would be wrong. Like most men of derring-do Blond really loved women. However he only ever made love to women who were ravishingly beautiful. Anything less and he just wasn't interested. Why settle for a Ford Focus when you can drive a Ferrari? Why eat beefburgers when you can dine on the finest Aberdeen Angus steak?

Still at the doorway Blond took in the room with a practised eye. It was quite obviously the apartment of a woman, but without being in the least 'girlie'. He certainly didn't envisage having to kick any cuddly toys off the bed when it came to having his way with the girl; that much was for certain. Bridget Jones she wasn't.

The large main room had quite obviously been designed by a decorator who knew his stuff, the money expended on the decor being self-evident; bright, clean lines, tasteful soft furnishings, unfussy furniture; Scandinavian by the look of it, but definitely a quantum leap up market from IKEA.

He noticed a Harry Potter book on a black glass-topped occasional table. From the doorway he couldn't make out the title, but guessed at 'Harry Potter and the Load of Old Bollocks'. As it was highly unlikely the girl was old enough to have a child of reading age it told him that in all probability she was reading the book herself. Blond smiled; excellent – he didn't like his lady friends to be too intelligent.

The girl became aware of him and gave a start, the involuntary hand going to her mouth too late to muffle a surprised little gasp.

Blond tipped an imaginary hat, bowed slightly from the neck and smiled. "Good evening."

"You!"

Though he had startled her the girl's voice was completely unafraid. Blond liked that - although he preferred his lady friends to be on the dimmer side of smart he did admire confidence in a woman, and this wonderful example of the species obviously had it in abundance.

The girl went on. "You were in the cocktail bar at Sandals."

Blond nodded. He closed the door behind him. "Allow me to introduce myself." He made his way over to her. "My name is James Blond." He reached out and took one of her hands in his. It was soft, velvety, the feel of lightly tanned skin, even though her skin was lily white. He fondled it for an instant, not wanting to let it go, before asking: "And you are, beautiful lady?"

"Pisa. Pisa Vass."

Blond smiled. "Pisa Vass. The name suits you."

Reluctantly he let go of the girl's hand and stepped back, the better to take in her appearance. He took his time about it. Her face, with its high cheekbones, wide-set eyes and the sort of full, red lips that could drive a man insane, was the sort of face that would always be beautiful. Of Eastern European extraction Blond guessed, with something of the Orient in there, Thai or Malayan possibly, which gave her features a distinctly exotic look. She was wearing a white silk shirt, tied at the waist, its neckline low and inviting, revealing just enough cleavage to get a man interested. Her black skirt, satisfyingly short, showed off her long legs to their best advantage. He wondered what she was wearing underneath. Nothing up top would be his guess - and he was usually right in these matters - and probably a G-string below, black, definitely black. Already Blond felt a stirring in his loins. Finally, after drinking richly from the vision before him he said: "When I first saw you I thought you were beautiful, Pisa, but close up you are beyond beauty."

She smiled, accepting the compliment without any sign of embarrassment, as if accustomed to such tributes to her beauty. She went to the expensive-looking bamboo and marble cocktail bar. Following her with his eyes Blond noticed over her shoulder that the door to the bedroom was open; a king-size silk-clad bed, mercifully clear of cuddly toys, beckoned invitingly. On one occasion, on the insistence of his lover, he'd had to share her bed with half the cast of The Muppets. Not surprisingly he found being watched by Kermit and Miss Piggy whilst performing the act of love to be such a disconcerting experience that at one point he almost lost his erection.

Now Pisa turned to him, refreshed her smile and said: "A drink, Mr Blond?"

"If it isn't too much trouble."

"I'm having a gin and tonic."

"I will take a dry Martini."

Pisa Vass poured the drinks and turned to Blond. "And, James Blond, as is the case with your fictitious near namesake James Bond, would you like it shaken?"

"Yes, but let's have a drink first," said Blond, mindful of his boss's wishes with regard to his coming out with witty lines whenever and wherever possible, good sense yielding to his inherent sense of duty.

He could see from Pisa's quick smile that the quip was not lost on her, but she merely nodded and handed him the drink. "Your dry Martini, Mr Blond."

He took the cool glass and looked straight into the eyes of the object of his affection. "Please, all my lovers call me James."

Pisa Vass returned his look, unblinkingly. "But I have never been your lover, Mr Blond."

She turned from him as if to walk away, but before she could he caught her lightly by the shoulders and applied just enough pressure to persuade her to turn to face him. "A state of affairs I am now going to take the greatest pleasure in rectifying," he said, permitting his hands to slide down her arms to encircle her slender waist. He nodded towards the bedroom. "Come, my lovely Pisa Vass."

"No." She pushed him away, not at all violently, but firmly enough to make it clear she meant what she said.

Blond was surprised to say the least. He raised a puzzled eyebrow. "No?"

"I can't."

His brow furrowed. "Can't? What do you mean, you can't?"

"I'm having my period."

"Having your period?"

"Yes. Sorry."

He was completely baffled. "But....I mean you can't be....the girls I meet are never having their period."

"Well I'm having mine," said Pisa, simply.

Blond simply couldn't credit it; for he was speaking the gospel truth. Just like the James Bond of book and film fame not once in his entire career had he encountered a girl who happened to be having her period when he came a calling; that sort of thing just didn't happen to famous secret agents.

The girl smiled pleasantly. "I could manage a hand job?"

Blond recoiled, visibly horrified at the suggestion. "A hand job?"

She made to pick up his glass. "Then let me at least freshen your Martini."

But Blond was in no mood to have his Martini freshened. A diplomatic exit was called for; to depart the girl's apartment now before he became even more disoriented, before he lost the plot completely. So without even considering a witty parting shot before making his exit, but with a final look of utter disbelief at the lovely Pisa Vass, he turned and left, perplexed, dismayed, shamefaced, embarrassed, all of those things. A minute later he stepped out of the apartment block and into the cold night air. It had started raining, making the evening almost as unwelcoming as Pisa Vass had been.

CHAPTER TWO

A NEW ASSIGNMENT

Two weeks later in Maddox's office, waiting for the arrival of his boss, James Blond turned his mind to the problem of the one-liners, the corny asides that Maddox now insisted Blond employ when on his assignments.

It had all started when Maddox, previously a rattling good second-in-command, had succeeded Pemberthy as head of MI6 a couple of months ago. Almost immediately Maddox had set about trying to raise the profile of the department. Some would argue, and did, that it might be preferable in view of the nature of its business for the department to keep a low profile, in fact the very name Secret Service suggests it, but Maddox didn't see it that way. This was almost certainly because he was a huge James Bond fan, and as such took a more romantic view of his profession than might be prudent for a man in his position. (On more than one occasion he had even been heard to refer to himself as 'M'.) Because of the similarity in names between the real secret agent James Blond and his fictitious counterpart James Bond, Maddox had thought it would be a good idea if Blond were to start behaving in the same manner as the movie icon. It would only be fitting, he had explained to Blond, as due to the enormously popular films the general public had come to expect secret service agents to behave in such a way.

In particular Maddox required him to come out with witty remarks at the drop of a hat, and especially so just before making an exit, a la 007. For his part Blond felt he had neither the time nor the inclination to dream up a stock of droll parting shots for his many assignments, and had argued as much with his boss. This had cut no ice whatsoever with Maddox, who had promptly engaged a scriptwriter to provide him with the necessary one-liners. However the venture had been far from a success, as the moment the scriptwriter had become a civil servant he had completely lost all his sense of humour.

In fact Maddox had once suggested to Blond in all seriousness that Ian Fleming, the creator of Bond, could very well have modelled his hero on Blond, citing the similarity of their names as the reason. Although Blond had openly ridiculed the idea he nevertheless had to admit to himself that Maddox's theory was not beyond the bounds of possibility, that he did indeed share a few similarities with the fictional secret agent. Their custom of having cigarettes etcetera especially made for them. Their good looks. Their fondness for the gaming tables. Certainly their penchant for beautiful women, along with the knack of picking them up. Although, unlike Bond, Blond had not had Pussy Galore, he had certainly had pussy galore. Last but not least their essential Britishness. But that was as far as it went. A few similarities, not a carbon copy. For one thing Bond didn't have problems with his prostate gland, Blond mused ruefully. Indeed as far as he could recall the fictional secret agent had never been to the lavatory once in any of the Bond books and films, let alone visited them with the frequency Blond found himself doing nowadays.

It was only because Maddox was otherwise excellent at his job that Blond had gone along with the idea, but that didn't mean he had to like it.

Notwithstanding his reservations, Blond was something of a fan of 007 himself, although by no means to the same extent as his boss. He particularly enjoyed the books. He wasn't as keen on the films, which he felt after the first three or four had become over-dependant on stunts and special effects at the expense of character. He had no criticism of the plots however, which some critics have claimed to be too fanciful or at best unrealistic; indeed he could cite several cases in which he had been involved, in particular the Singh Singh and the Doctor Zog affairs, which on the face of it were much more far-fetched than any case that James Bond had ever been assigned to; indeed arch villains and fancifulness seemed to come hand in hand with each other. As for the actors chosen to play the part of Bond, once Sean Connery had quit the role, well the less said about those the better, although this Daniel Craig chap looked quite promising. Blond too.

Now, waiting for Maddox to put in an appearance, Blond had every intention of making it clear to his boss that he had grown tired of the charade and would have nothing further to do with it. He conjectured as to how he might set about this, the head of MI6 not being the sort of man to whom you refused to obey a direct order unless you had a damned good reason.

The office had changed little since Blond had first entered it all those missions ago. A sparsely but comfortably furnished room; a large oak desk on which sat a silver gilt-framed photograph of Maddox's family, an antique onyx inkwell and pens, three telephones, two black one red, the latter a direct link to No 10 Downing Street; a couple of green filing cabinets; three comfortable brown leather-upholstered chairs in addition to the one behind Maddox's desk; an Axminster carpet that had seen better days; a hat stand.

The door suddenly opened and Maddox entered, bringing Blond out of his reverie. The Head of MI6 was still tanned from a recent holiday in the Canary Islands and looked as fit as a fiddle in his charcoal grey suit, crisp white shirt and polka-dot tie. A matching handkerchief poking out of his breast pocket completed the ensemble. Blond could see from his demeanour that his boss was in a foul mood. "I've been told to take on a woman for God's sake!" said Maddox, as he crossed the room to his desk.

Blond forgot his own problems for the moment. "A woman secret agent you mean?"

Maddox nodded as he took his seat. "The powers-that-be have decided that without a woman the department is politically incorrect. Have you ever heard of anything so damned stupid?"

Blond hadn't. What's more, he could see a problem immediately, for, from being a man who never thought about women having periods, since the episode with Pisa Vass he had scarcely thought about anything else. "What about their periods?" he scoffed. "You can't take a week off every month in this game just because you're feeling a bit off."

Thrown this potential lifeline Maddox brightened considerably. "Good point, James. I'll put that to the blighters."

A little happier now Maddox started to go down Tobacco Road, the name given by one of Blond's compatriots to the long and tortuous route that Maddox took in the process of lighting his pipe. "Incidentally, what's the latest on the old prostate, James?" he now asked, between misguidedly ambitious puffs on his ancient briar.

Blond scowled on being reminded of his little problem. "About the same, sir."

"Dodgy waterworks not interfering with your work then?"

"Not at all," Blond lied.

"You really ought to get it fixed, you know. One thing's for certain, it won't get any better by itself. SA-5 had the same problem not so long back; had a simple operation at St Bart's, in and out in a couple of days, week's convalescence and now he's as right as ninepence."

"I'll think about it, sir."

It was doubtful in the extreme that Blond would think about it, and even if he did it would only be to come up with even more ways of avoiding the operation rather than to advance any plans to expedite it.

Blond, for a man who sometimes killed with cold steel, had a mortal fear of surgery. But perhaps the reason he had such strong reservations on the advisability or otherwise of such a procedure was because he employed cold steel in his profession. He knew only too well what it was capable of, especially if it happened to be a scalpel operating on a prostate gland, and how one small slip could put a premature end to a chap's love life.

Maddox got his pipe going at last. "So then SA-Seven, to business." He referred to the dossier on his desk, "Your next assignment." His earnest grey eyes regarded Blond. "There's a character by the name of Dr Goldnojaws we want you to take a look at."

Blond's ears pricked. "Dr Goldnojaws?"

"And his assistant, BloJob."

"BloJob? He sounds like a really nasty piece of work."

"She."

"She sounds really interesting."

Maddox frowned and shook his head. "She's not one for you I'm afraid, SA-Seven."

Blond was disappointed. "Fat is she? Or plain perhaps?" Blond was particularly indifferent to women who were unfortunate enough to have been born plain or disinterested enough in their appearance to have allowed themselves to run to fat.

To add weight to his words Maddox paused slightly before answering. "She is evil incarnate, James. You remember Oddjob in the Bond film Dr No?"

"Of course."

"Well what Oddjob did with his bowler hat BloJob does with her brassiere."

"She wears a bra on her head?"

Maddox looked puzzled. "Wears a bra on her head?"

"Just joking, sir."

"Good man. Remember to use that ploy whenever you're making an exit and you won't go far wrong."

Blond groaned. He had been hopeful that Maddox might have forgotten about the one-liner nonsense and now he'd reminded him of it. Why couldn't he keep his big mouth shut?

"However BloJob's bra is not a thing to joke about, James," Maddox went on. "You see she uses it as a weapon. Fills the cups with large cannonballs and uses it like a bolas. I have it on good authority she once brought down a buffalo at two hundred paces."

Blond was impressed. "That good, eh?" With some difficulty he dragged his attention away from the thought of a buffalo being brought to its knees by a cannonball-filled flying bra and back to the matter at hand. "So then, what manner of evil has this character Dr Goldnojaws been up to?"

Maddox paused before saying, with the timbre of awe in his voice: "Nothing short of total Stockport domination SA-Seven!"

Blond wasn't at all sure he'd heard Maddox correctly. "I'm sorry, did you say Stockport domination?"

"Thought you'd be impressed, James," said Maddox, disingenuously substituting the disbelief in Blond's reply in favour of enthusiasm. "Yes, apparently it is our friend Dr Goldnojaws' aim to dominate Stockport. And it will be your job to see that he doesn't succeed."

Blond sat back in his chair and considered Maddox's proposition. "I see." The tone of his voice indicated that he was less than enthusiastic.

"You seem a mite disappointed, James?"

"Well I am, sir. And no bones about it. Usually the criminals and villains I'm asked to deal with are intent on nothing short of world domination."

Maddox's tone was conciliatory. "Yes I'm aware of that SA-Seven; but at the moment we have only one case on the books in which someone is intent on achieving nothing short of world domination and I gave it to SA-Three. I did think of you for the assignment, I must admit, in fact I would have preferred you, but apparently there will be a lot of legwork involved - and with your waterworks problem..."

Blond, deeply offended, immediately sprang to his defence. "My waterworks problem in no way interferes with my ability to carry out my job as a secret agent! Sir!"

Maddox took his time before replying. Blond was a top agent, the department's best, and he didn't want to alienate him any more than he had already. Finally he said in measured tones: "James on your last but one job you lost the trail of the man you were tailing because you had to go to the lavatory."

"Sir, I…"

Maddox butted in, before Blond could go any further. "And there's no point in your denying it SA-Seven, SA-Fourteen was on the case with you and felt it was his duty to report it to me."

"I wasn't going to deny it. The reason I had to go to the lavatory was a dodgy curry, courtesy of Singh Singh, not my prostate gland."

"Be that as it may, the decision has been made." He remembered something. "Oh and by the by, our friend Postlethwaite has come up with something that could very well help you to take on cases that need a lot of legwork, which he'll no doubt brief you on when you see him immediately you've finished with me, but in the meantime…." He raised his eyebrows pointedly. "So you're happy with that, James?" Maddox's tone of voice indicated he was not seeking Blond's approval but firmly putting his foot down.

Blond gave a long-suffering sigh. "Very well, sir."

"Good." Maddox went on. "So then, to this Stockport business. Incidentally have you ever been there? Stockport?"

"I've managed to resist the temptation until now."

"Then you're an excellent judge. Frightful place. I spent a day there once. It was like two weeks without a woman. Not that you'd be interested in the women of Stockport. Ugly?" Maddox pulled a face.

"Thanks for the tip."

"As the actress said to the bishop." Maddox chuckled. "Thanks for the tip! Good one, eh?"

Blond suspected that the scriptwriter brought in to supply him with one-liners had also been supplying Maddox with them, but laughed politely.

Maddox smiled. "That's better, James. That's more like the SA-Seven we know and love. Now then, this Dr Goldnojaws character. Apparently he's set up a shoe manufacturing company in Stockport which trades under the name of Façade. Which we're fairly sure it is."

"Sir?"

"A façade. We suspect he's using the place as a front for whatever nefarious business he's up to."

"I'm absolutely sure he is, sir," said Blond, confidently.

"James?"

Blond explained. "His name, Dr Goldnojaws; and that of his accomplice, BloJob. You haven't noticed anything unusual about them?"

Maddox frowned. "Unusual?"

"Their names are portmanteau words. Invented words. In this instance made up from the names of villains in the James Bond films – Goldfinger, Dr No and Jaws; Blofeld and Oddjob."

With a gasp of surprise Maddox now saw the connection. "By Jove, so they are! I hadn't twigged that at all. Well done SA-Seven!"

"And unless I'm very much mistaken the names have been made up by this Dr Goldnojaws character with the express purpose of cocking a snook at the Secret Service. For the same warped reason that he's called his shoe factory Façade."

Maddox looked puzzled. "But why? Why would a villain intent on committing a crime deliberately draw attention to himself?"

"I have no idea, sir. But I intend to find out."

"Good chap. Excellent." Maddox's pipe had gone out and he started out on the long road to getting it going again before he continued. "You won't know much about Stockport I take it?"

"Very little except that it's in the north-west of England and thus probably very wet. Sale Sharks play there now I believe. Rugger. That's about the sum total of my knowledge of the place."

"Thought that might be the case. So I've arranged for someone to fill you in when you arrive there. Tell you all about its charms. Should take all of two minutes from what I remember of it, but you never know. Anyway you're to meet up with him, a Mr Medlock, at the Town Hall tomorrow morning."

Blond could feel a cloak of boredom wrapping itself around him already. "Will that be absolutely necessary, sir?"

"I'm afraid so, James. There must be some reason why Goldnojaws wants to dominate such a Godforsaken hole as Stockport and once you know a little more about it you might just be able to put your finger on it."

"You can count on me, sir."

Maddox regarded Blond fondly. "I know I can, SA-Seven. Off you trot then."

Blond made no move to leave. Maddox looked inquiringly at him. "Was there something else, James?"

"About the one-liners, sir. Which I'm not at all happy about, as you know. I…"

But Maddox butted in before Blond could state his objections. "Glad you brought that up, James. Have a word with Postlethwaite about it. He's sorted something out for you. I think you'll be pleased."

Blond didn't think he'd be at all pleased.

CHAPTER THREE

A SLIGHT HITCH

Quickly dropping his trousers and allowing them to fall round his ankles in the men's toilet at the Tesco superstore Blond cursed Postlethwaite for the umpteenth time that day. Things had started to go wrong from the moment he had entered Postlethwaite's office following his briefing by Maddox.

Over the years SA-Seven had visited the office of the Secret Service's quartermaster almost as often as he'd visited Maddox's. It was where he picked up the tools of his trade. And what tools they were; devilishly clever tools dreamed up by Postlethwaite's team of top boffins; shoes with false heels where anything from phials of poison to emergency currency could be secreted; a jacket whose narrow lapels held a six inch stiletto and a skeleton key that could open any lock yet devised by man; a gun that looked like a cigarette lighter; and, on one occasion, and intended only as an amusing conversation piece, a cigarette lighter that looked like a gun, and which had unfortunately been responsible for the demise of agent SA-Thirteen when he had pulled it out to offer a light to a member of the Chicago Mafia.

"Come in, come in, SA-Seven," Postlethwaite, full of his usual bonhomie, called to Blond as the secret agent entered, "I have some rather good news for you."

"Yes?"

Postlethwaite smiled. "Yes it's about the one-liners." Blond's face fell. How could this be good news? Postlethwaite went on. "We had to get rid of the fellow we engaged as he was obviously not up to the standard required."

"I've heard funnier funeral services," Blond commented, dryly.

"Quite." Postlethwaite looked inquiringly at Blond. "Did you ever see 'Blind Date', SA-Seven? It's a TV show. Was a TV show. About ten years back, not on any more."

"I'm not surprised."

"You saw it then?"

"I once had that unfortunate experience, yes. For about two minutes. I seem to remember some screeching Liverpudlian harpy with a laugh like a demented hyena."

"That's the show. Right. So I'd better fill you in then if that's all you've seen of it. Basically it's a sort of dating show. The idea is that the man, or 'guy' as he is often called, has to choose a partner from a selection of three girls. Now he can't see the girls, they're behind a screen, hence 'Blind Date', and the chap has to pick a mate on the basis of the girls' replies to his questions. He says something like 'I'm into cricket in a big way so why should I choose you, Girl Number One?' and she replies with something like 'Because with me on your side you're bound to bowl a maiden over', or maybe 'Because I'm just the girl to draw your stumps', that sort of thing. All terribly smutty. And all heavily scripted of course. Well the thing is, I've managed to acquire the services of one of the show's scriptwriters to pen your one-liners. Apparently he's been struggling for work since the show folded. Can't think why, he's excellent."

Blond made no effort to keep the sarcasm out of his voice. "And that's good news? That I'm to have the benefit of witticisms written by someone who dreams up such lines as 'I'm just the girl to draw your stumps'?"

"Well I can't guarantee they'll all be as good as that."

Blond made a mental note to put even more sarcasm into his voice in his future dealings with Postlethwaite as the large helping he'd just used had obviously not been enough.

The quartermaster then produced a crescent-shaped piece of transparent plastic, about four inches long and maybe half an inch wide, rather like a piece of flexible plastic piping cut in half. "I've got this for you."

Blond was intrigued. "What is it?"

"A stiff upper lip," said Postlethwaite, then added, obviously pleased with himself. "One of my own ideas, actually."

Blond looked puzzled. "A stiff upper lip?"

"For whenever you find yourself in a tight corner."

Blond pointed out the obvious. "Postlethwaite, as a British Secret Agent I already have a stiff upper lip; it is a prerequisite for anyone who aspires to the job."

The quartermaster smiled conspirationally. "You haven't got one like this little beauty SA-Seven. It's rather special if I may say so." He held out the contraption in the palm of his hand so Blond could take a closer look at it. "No ordinary plastic, this. Plastic explosive."

"Plastic explosive?"

"The idea is that when you are about to fall into enemy hands, with all the concomitant nasty things that such an unfortunate occurrence would entail, you simply bite on your stiff upper lip and......poof!"

"I turn into a homosexual?"

"What? No, 'poof' the thing explodes. Bang! Much better than a cyanide pill I'm sure you'll agree."

Blond immediately spotted at least one fly in the ointment. "And what if I manage to break out of enemy hands and on my way to escaping I happen to stumble and bite on this stiff upper lip gizmo by accident?"

Postlethwaite put on his honest, earnest face. "Well I'd be lying to you if I said that couldn't happen, James."

"You would be taking the piss out of me if you said it couldn't happen, Postlethwaite," said Blond with feeling. "Not to put too fine a point on it."

The quartermaster was ruffled. "There's no need for that sort of talk, old boy. We're all of us doing our best I'm sure."

Blond could see no benefit in pursuing the matter further so moved on. "Maddox intimated you had something which might help me with my prostate problem? Not that it's giving me much trouble nowadays."

Postlethwaite's eyes lit up, the previous disagreement forgotten about immediately. "My piece de resistance, James." He went over to a filing cabinet, opened the top drawer and produced a weird-looking contraption that closely resembled a colostomy bag with a five inch by two inch flexible rubber spout attached to it. He held it up for Blond's approval, smiling as might a gardener holding up a prize-winning vegetable.

Blond blinked. "What on earth......?"

"A urine collector," said Postlethwaite, with even more pride in his voice than when he had introduced Blond to the stiff upper lip. "Here's the way it works. You insert your penis in here, so." He put his finger in the spout. "Press this button here." He pressed a red button on a small box of tricks attached to the side of the plastic bag. "And the walls of the spout close gently in, trapping your John Thomas firmly but comfortably. The capacity is a half of one imperial gallon and it's absolutely one hundred per cent safe. On that point you can be fully assured," he emphasised. "We've tested it on animals."

"Animals?"

"A donkey to be precise. Did forty trips up and down Brighton beach without batting an eyelid."

Blond suspected that anyone seeing the donkey trotting up and down Brighton beach with what looked like a colostomy bag dangling from its dick might well have batted the odd eyelid, but refrained from saying so. Instead he took the urine collector from Postlethwaite and looked at it more closely. Certainly if he were to wear it he wouldn't have to take time out to relieve himself quite so often, but even so....

Postlethwaite broke in to his thoughts. "Made from specially toughened plastic with fibre glass impregnated into it so that there's absolutely no chance of it bursting. We've tested it, the sharpest knife won't even scratch it, much less penetrate it," he went on. "And to release it you simply press the red button twice. The donkey couldn't get the hang of that but I'm quite sure you will SA-Seven, being much more intelligent than a donkey of course. However the best part is to come."

Blond could hardly wait. "And that is?"

"It turns your urine into heavy water."

"Heavy water?"

"High explosive."

"I wasn't asking what heavy water is, I know full well what it is and what it is capable of," Blond said, tetchily, "I was doubting the wisdom of such a metamorphosis."

Postlethwaite chose to ignore Blond's criticism of his department's brainchild and continued: "Then, when the process has taken place, about ten minutes, instead of having say a pint of urine in it you have half a pint of top quality heavy water; enough to blow up a small factory. And I can't stress too much how useful that might be in an emergency."

Blond made sure he'd got it absolutely correct. "So what you're saying in effect is that I'll be going about my everyday business with up to half a gallon of heavy water hanging down the inside of my trousers?"

"Well that's one way of looking at it."

"Which could explode at any moment?"

The quartermaster began to hedge. "Well, technically I suppose that could happen."

"Yes well I don't think I'll bother if it's all the same to you."

Postlethwaite's face fell. "Really? The lads will be most disappointed, they've put a lot of hours in on this one."

Blond made to leave. "So if that's the best you can do I will wish you good day."

Postlethwaite held up a restraining hand. "No, hold on. I want you to have this." From his pocket he produced a wrist watch, which he held up for Blond's approval.

"I already have a watch thank you very much," said Blond, sniffily.

"Not like this one you haven't. It's atomic."

"Atomic?"

"Precisely."

"I see. So if the stiff upper lip doesn't blow my head off and the urine collector doesn't blow my bollocks off the atomic wristwatch will blow my hand off."

Postlethwaite shrugged off this latest objection easily. "No, James, you misunderstand. It's not atomic as in bomb, it's atomic as in precision timepiece that measures time by using the regular oscillation of individual atoms or molecules to regulate its movement. Completely safe I can assure you. And on the subject of safety, what do you think of this?" He flipped open the back of the watch. In the back, a perfect fit, was a rolled-up condom. "For emergencies," Postlethwaite smiled.

Blond regarded it. It was the first half-decent idea Postlethwaite had come up with during the entire interview.

*

Now, in the Tesco men's toilets, Blond quickly slipped the battery into the urine collector and pressed the red button once. He grunted with a mixture of satisfaction and relief as it immediately began to emit a low hum. He pressed the red button twice more in quick succession and mercifully the rubber spout released its grip on his penis. He breathed easily for the first time in hours. So far so good. Now what he needed, and most urgently, was a pee. But the security guards were already hammering on the door, a door Blond noted was of such flimsy construction that it wouldn't be much longer before they succeeded in breaking it down.

"Come on out of there, you can't get away feller," called one of the security guards.

"And don't try any funny business, there's two of us," added the second.

Blond smiled to himself at the incongruity of the statement. Two Tesco security guards indeed! In circumstances not too dissimilar to the one in which he now found himself he had once made good his escape from seven Red Army guards and four Rottweilers and had still found time to light a Sobranie while he was doing it. Two underpaid and probably overweight Tesco security guards weren't going to trouble him too much. In fact not at all, Blond thought, as he now noticed an outside window set high in the wall. It was small, but not so small that a man couldn't crawl through it.

But first things first. He took hold of his newly-released penis, directed it at the lavatory pan, and with a huge sigh of relief peed for England.

Hearing the flow of the urine one of the security guards said: "Can you hear that Dwayne? The cheeky twat's having a piss!"

"Cheeky twat!" echoed Dwayne, equally affronted. He started pounding on the door again.

Blond, taking offence at being called a cheeky twat, decided to show them just how cheeky a twat he could be and directed a jet of pee over the top of the door. There was an unbelieving and immediate bellow of anger from the other side. "The cheeky twat's pissed on me!" Followed by further pounding on the door. "Let's have you out of there right this minute you dirty bastard, I'll show you if you'll piss on my uniform!"

For good measure Blond now tossed the urine collector over the top of the door. It must have landed on either Dwayne or his mate as almost immediately there was a shriek and a cry of "Aaaaaagh, get it off me!" the security man possibly thinking it was a close relative of the thing that burst out of John Hurt's stomach to such shocking effect in the film 'Alien'. Judging by the reaction it wasn't having a much less dramatic result.

By now Blond had pulled up his trousers and was standing on the lavatory seat and opening the window.

Seconds later he dropped and landed lightly on his feet outside. He quickly took his bearings and hurried off in the direction of the Lada.

The Lada had made the drive north a nightmare. Blond himself had contributed to the nightmare in no little way, as rather injudiciously for a man with a prostate problem about to set out on a long journey by car he had drunk two large cups of coffee with his English breakfast in addition to his usual half pint of freshly-squeezed orange juice. That alone would have been enough but it was a bitterly cold morning and the Lada's heater had packed up. Consequentially Blond had to keep stopping to relieve himself. After calling in at the third motorway service station in a row he hit upon a solution to the problem. He would put the urine collector to good purpose.

At Postlethwaite's insistence he had brought the device along with him. Not that he had any intention of ever wearing it; he valued his manhood far too much for that. However it had occurred to him that if he were to disconnect the heavy water processing part of the contraption he could then use it simply as something to pee in, a sort of mobile mini-lavatory. This he did, by first putting it on and then discarding the battery, thus rendering the heavy water element of it defunct. All had gone well, and he had already had two satisfying pees in it. However shortly after reaching the outskirts of Stockport trouble struck when the Lada broke down. The cause of the breakdown was a lack of water in the car's cooling system which had caused the radiator to run dry. The irony, that the radiator had run dry due to a lack of water whilst he had a goodly supply of it on tap as it were, and would merely have had to keep peeing in the radiator to keep it topped up, was not lost on Blond, but it was too late for that now, and by the time he had managed to get a garage to effect a repair it was approaching nightfall.

After checking in at the Cheshire Towers, which was the nearest thing Stockport had to a decent hotel, and not all

that near to it in Blond's opinion, he refreshed himself
before attempting to take off the urine collector, which
was by now quite full, courtesy of the several cups of coffee
he'd consumed whilst waiting for the car to be repaired.
He pressed the red button twice, as instructed by
Postlethwaite, but nothing happened. He tried once more.
Again, nothing. He cursed under his breath as he realised
that when he'd removed the battery, thus getting rid of the
power source that processed the heavy water, he had
inadvertently also got rid of the power source which
opened and closed the spout that was firmly clamped round
his penis. And he'd thrown the battery away! Not only that,
he now needed another pee and the bag was full.

He would have to get in touch with Postlethwaite, there
was nothing else for it. His bladder by now seemingly
bursting, for there is nothing that makes a man with a
prostate problem want a pee more than the fact he can't
have one, he phoned Postlethwaite on his mobile. Having
had to be called to the phone it took some time for
Postlethwaite to answer and when he did he was more than
a trifle annoyed. "Dash it all, I'm in the middle of dinner,"
he complained. "Who is that?"

Blond, although desperate to rid himself of the urine
collector, still observed strict protocol. He therefore spoke
in a language he knew Postlethwaite would understand but
that anyone listening in to them wouldn't have a clue as to
what they were talking about. "This is the Northern
Courier," he began. "Arrived safely in Grotland. The
waterworks there isn't all that it should be and the
equipment recently installed to put it right is in urgent need
of repair. Please advise."

"What?" said Postlethwaite, sounding a bit puzzled.

Blond remained calm, and repeated, more slowly: "This
is the Northern Courier. Arrived safely in Grotland. The
waterworks there isn't all that it should be and the
equipment recently installed to put it right is in urgent need
of repair. Please advise."

"What's that you say?" barked Postlethwaite, testily, "What on earth are you rambling on about man?"

Blond snapped. "It's Blond, I'm in Stockport, and your bloody urine collector is stuck on my cock!" he bellowed down the phone.

"There's no need to shout, I'm not deaf," complained the affronted voice on the other end of the phone. "Stuck in what way?"

"In the way that I can't get it off my cock, you stupid sod, in what way do you think?" Blond spat out. "The spout won't open up when I press the red button twice."

There was silence for a second or two, then Postlethwaite said thoughtfully: "Could be the battery I suppose. The donkey might have ran it down a little more than I thought."

Blond hadn't until that moment realised that the urine collector he was wearing and the one worn by the donkey were one and the same and now that he did he didn't care for it one little bit. However now was not the time to start complaining about his penis having shared the same sheath as a member of the animal kingdom. He thought quickly. What to do? He certainly didn't want to admit to Postlethwaite that he'd discarded the battery. There was nothing for it, he would have to lie, it went against the grain but needs must. "You're right," he said, "I've just checked the battery and it's completely dead."

Postlethwaite's nonchalant tone informed him that in his opinion Blond's situation wasn't the end of the world. "No matter, you'll simply have to replace it. That shouldn't be a problem, it's a normal watch battery, use the one in your watch."

Blond breathed an audible sigh of relief. "Will....." He was about to follow the 'Will' with a 'do', but then remembered something. "Damn!"

"What's the matter?"

"I can't."

"Why not?"

"I'm not wearing my usual watch. I'm wearing the atomic watch you gave me."

"Well then you'll just have to go out and buy a battery, won't you," said Postlethwaite, and promptly put down the phone, cutting short anything further Blond might have to say on the subject.

Blond, who hadn't cried since he was a child of fourteen, when he'd fractured his arm on falling out of a tree, was now very close to tears, for by this time he was in severe pain. In desperation he tried to urinate into the already full bag - surely it would take a little bit more, enough to ease the pain just a little, give him a bit of breathing space? But it wouldn't, for no sooner had he begun to pee than it started backing up. He stopped trying immediately, fearing that more pee might go back up his penis than had come out of it and make the pain even worse than it already was. In desperation, and although Postlethwaite had told him that the plastic bag was one hundred per cent indestructible, Blond tried to cut through it with his penknife. He quickly gave up when the razor-sharp blade of the knife slipped off the diamond hard plastic and narrowly missed his testicles. There was nothing else for it, he would have to go out and buy a battery.

If Blond had wanted a Chinese takeaway he could have had his choice from a dozen outlets. Likewise Indian takeaways, along with several Thai and two Malaysian. He could have purchased kebabs, both doner and shish, pizzas with more toppings than you could shake a stick at; Big Macs and Kentucky Fried Chicken could be had, along with fish and chips plus whatever other delights fish and chip shops purveyed; petrol could be bought both in its leaded and unleaded forms, along with diesel and oil; cinemas could be visited; bingo could be played; pubs with their beer, wine, spirits, potato crisps and pork scratchings could be dropped in on; and Stockport County supporters dressed in football shirts and scarves hurrying along the pavements suggested that football could be watched at

Edgeley Park, where no doubt burgers, hot dogs, pies, tea, coffee and Oxo could be bought. But could a battery for a watch be bought? Apparently not. Granted it was by now turned seven-o-clock, but one would have thought that there would be at least one shop open that sold watch batteries. But any likely outlet, a jewellers, perhaps a newsagents, certainly an electrical shop, had by then had their doors locked, their graffiti-emblazoned shutters pulled down and secured.

By now quite desperate, Blond had actually parked up the Lada, entered an Indian takeaway, and asked the man behind the counter if he possibly had a battery. The man nodded eagerly, smiled most pleasantly, disappeared into the back and returned two minutes later with a balti. Blond had no more success when he went into the next kebab house he came across and asked the same question, only for the dusky individual behind the counter to tell him to "Get out of here before I call the bloody police, and bloody quick about it man, bloody trouble causer bugger sod."

Cruising the streets again Blond now chanced upon a Tesco store. A very large Tesco store. A hypermarket in fact. Surely a store of such size would sell watch batteries? God knows supermarkets seemed to sell just about everything else these days.

And that was what he found, on entering the store and asking the first assistant he came across; that they sold just about everything else these days but watch batteries.

On discovering this Blond became quite desperate, for he had never known such agony in his life. Then, out of the blue, he had a brainwave. Yes! Of course! It could only have been due to the excruciating pain fogging up his brain and preventing it from functioning properly that he hadn't thought of it before. He would simply ask someone for the loan of their watch battery. And what could be more simple? For there were still plenty of shoppers in the store, even at eight-thirty in the evening. Some of them would be bound to be wearing watches. But how to go about it?

Blond knew that if he were to spin someone a yarn there was a danger he wouldn't be believed, and if the person didn't believe him they certainly wouldn't offer him the loan of their watch battery. He decided on the truth; the British way; the truth always paid in the long run. Taking the bull by the horns he approached a mild-looking man and said: "My name is Blond. James Blond. I'm here in Stockport to check out the mysterious Dr Goldnojaws and his henchwoman BloJob who are intent on nothing less than complete Stockport domination. I have a urine collector stuck on my penis due to battery failure so I would like to borrow your watch battery if I may, so that I might free myself."

"Fuck off you weirdo," said the man, after looking Blond up and down suspiciously for a couple of seconds. He then turned his back on him and walked away muttering "Must think I dropped off a bloody flitting or something."

So much for the truth, thought Blond. But before he could bemoan his luck any further an opportunity suddenly presented itself, a way out of his dilemma. Thank heaven for little girls, Blond said to himself, for as well as getting bigger every day they also invariably trail several yards behind their mother when she is shopping in a supermarket, and one such little girl was doing that very thing at this very moment and not a yard from where he was standing. More importantly she was wearing a watch. Blond bent over to speak to her and in his best avuncular manner said: "Hello, little girl."

The little girl, a blue-eyed, pert-nosed, heart-breaking beauty of the future, eyed him suspiciously, as little girls, their mothers having warned them never to speak to strangers, are wont to do.

"Don't be afraid," said Blond, taking a surreptitious look up the aisle to check if the child's mother was still engrossed in making her selection of which brand of baked beans in tomato sauce to buy. She was. He smiled at the little girl. "What's your name?"

The little girl shrugged off enough of her suspicion to answer. "Hayley. What's yours?"

"Thanks for asking, I'll have a pint of bitter."

As well as insisting he take the urine collector with him on his travels Postlethwaite had also insisted that Blond take the hundred one-liners the ex-Blind Date scriptwriter had penned for him thus far. Despite his personal opinion regarding his employing witticisms at the drop of a hat, to help take his mind off the fact that he desperately want a pee Blond had committed most of the one-liners to memory during the journey to Stockport. When the opportunity presented itself the line had sprung to mind and from there to his lips quite automatically. And in the event quite fortunately, as it dispelled any lingering suspicions the little girl may have harboured. She now wrinkled her nose, smiled at Blond, and said: "You're funny."

Yes and I'm also desperate for a pee, thought Blond, but said: "Sorry about that. My name is James Blond. That's a nice watch you're wearing, Hayley."

It couldn't have gone better if Blond had choreographed it himself. Hayley held out her arm, inviting Blond to take a closer look at the watch. He quickly grabbed her hand, tore the watch from her wrist and was legging it for the nearby gents' toilet in a flash. Hayley immediately started to scream blue murder. Alarmed, her mother raced to her side. Hayley stopped screaming for long enough to burble to her mother what had happened and to thrust an accusing finger in Blond's direction. But by then he was at the door with the little man painted on it that offered sanctuary.

As Blond entered the toilets he saw from the corner of his eye that the attention of a security guard had been alerted. He would have to be quick. And then he would have to find a means of escape; the very last thing he wanted was a clash with the local constabulary and a possible charge of child abuse.

*

Now, safe in the Lada, or as safe as it is possible to be in a Lada, Blond drove out of the Tesco car park and pointed the aged car in the direction of the Cheshire Towers. He was already feeling much better, but he would feel even better still once he'd got a good meal and a decent bottle of burgundy inside him.

CHAPTER FOUR

KARAOKE

The time was ten minutes after nine when Blond finally made it back to the Cheshire Towers. He was not so naïve as to think the hotel would still be serving dinner at that hour. This was not, after all, the south of France or the West Indies or Mexico or any other of the exotic foreign climes where SA-Seven's assignments usually took him, countries where a hungry man could walk into any hotel which took his fancy at ten in the evening and order dinner; this was England, a country where such a request could only lead to the requester being regarded as either someone coming from another planet, having a laugh or simply being stark raving mad.

But a sandwich perhaps? Surely that wouldn't be asking too much. Nothing special, nothing too complicated, not a demand for hot pastrami and dill pickle on rye with a rocket and aioli dressing; a simple ham or cheese sandwich would do admirably. Not to be. The chances of getting such a sandwich at the Cheshire Towers hotel at ten past nine in the evening were as remote as Pluto. Quite impossible, he had been informed by the receptionist; the chef had finished for the evening. Well could the receptionist herself perhaps make him a sandwich? Certainly not, the very idea, was he joking, what did he think she was? She was a receptionist, not a cook. Besides she'd just had her nails done and apart from that the chef had locked the fridge and gone home.

Blond might have offered to open the lock of the fridge with his universal skeleton key and in a matter of moment make available the delights to be found within, but that would only have drawn attention to himself - the very last thing a secret agent wished to do. So he persisted with his grilling of the totally disinterested receptionist. Did the hotel perhaps boast a snack dispenser where bars of chocolate and potato crisps could be obtained? Yes, it did. Two in fact. Where in the hotel could they be located? One just round the corner next to the lift, the other at the top of the steps leading to the first floor. But the former was empty, the man who filled it hadn't called this week, he was on holiday, and the latter had broken down three weeks ago and was still awaiting repair.

On being told this Blond had given up the ghost and left the hotel to seek out the nearest pub. About two minutes after finding it he began to wish he had sought out the second nearest pub as it surely must have been better than the one he'd fetched up in. Up to the two minute mark it hadn't been too bad, a little more untidy than he would have liked – he didn't much care for the beer-stained bar top, nor indeed the cat sitting on it - but nothing that couldn't be tolerated by a man desperate for sustenance.

On entering the pub he had gone to the bar and ordered a pint of bitter and a pork pie. The pie had yet to arrive but he had been assured by the landlord that when it did arrive it would be of excellent quality; Titterton's, made locally, none better in his opinion, the cat loved them, wouldn't eat anything else, turned its nose up at Wall's. The beer was excellent too, the landlord further advised him, Robinson's best bitter; real ale, brewed less than a couple of hundred yards down the road at the famed Unicorn Brewery.

Blond wrapped a hand round the thick, dimpled pint pot favoured in that part of the country and took a draught of the foaming beer that seconds earlier the landlord had set down before him. Mine Host was right, the brew was excellent. Blond was glad that at least the people of Stockport had good beer to drink since from what he'd seen of the town so far he had formed the opinion that the only way to cope with living in it would be to maintain a constant state of inebriation.

He thought he might have at least one more pint, maybe two, to wash down the pie when it came, but suddenly his evening began to go pear-shaped. Raising the pint pot to his lips to take another drink he almost dropped it in surprise when an ear-splitting screech that must have been something in the order of ninety decibels suddenly assaulted his eardrums.

At first I was afraid, I was petrified......

"What the..." spluttered Blond, a cataract of Robinson's best bitter cascading from his mouth and down his chin, wetting his shirt front and tie.

"Karaoke night," said the landlord, rolling his eyes.

"Karaoke?" Blond had heard of the phenomenon of karaoke but had never experienced it until now.

"Every Thursday," said the Landord, then added mischievously, having noted Blond's reaction to the first line of Gloria Gaynor's hit 'I Will Survive', "You're in luck."

The singer, for want of a better expression, was in another room further up the passage, and sounded about as much like the famed American chanteuse she was attempting to impersonate as Mickey Mouse with laryngitis sounds like the late Pavarotti.

Go on now go walk out the door
Just turn around now
'cause you're not welcome anymore......

"I don't know about anybody not being welcome anymore but she certainly isn't welcome here anymore," said the landlord, with some feeling, nodding in the direction of the singing. "Every bloody week she's here.

Same bloody song. 'I Will Survive'. I mean I could do with it if it was just her but no, I get at least four of 'em singing it. I had eight one week. I tried fooling them once, I rigged the karaoke machine so when you pressed 'I Will Survive' the words and music for 'God Save The Queen' came on but it didn't make any difference, they still sang 'I Will Survive'."

"It's anthemic," said a small man at the bar, sagely.

"What?"

"Women look upon it as their anthem," the man explained. "A homage to womanhood. The survival of woman in a man's world. My wife used to sing 'I Will Survive' all the time."

"Used to?" said Blond.

"She died."

"Didn't survive then, did she," said the landlord, unnecessarily and a little hurtful in Blond's opinion. The landlord went on: "No, I'm a man who normally wouldn't wish death on my worst enemy, but I dearly wish that bugger singing won't survive for much longer."

Blond listened to the woman with a horrible fascination. Wondering what she looked like he now made his way up the passage to where the sound was coming from and looked through the open doorway.

The room, maybe fifty feet by forty, was packed. There must have been a hundred people in it, maybe more, most of whom were seated at small round tables or bench seats set against the flock-wallpapered walls, a few of them dancing on the postage stamp-sized dance floor in front of the tiny corner stage. There were about as many women as there were men. By far the most popular drink was pints of beer, for both sexes. Amazingly, given the standard of entertainment on offer, they all appeared to be having the time of their lives, especially the women.

Looking at the women now Blond reflected that when Maddox had called them ugly he'd been a little hard on the female population of Stockport. Their behaviour was ugly certainly, swigging pints of beer in a manner that wouldn't disgrace a docker on pay day, laughing raucously the while.

Women didn't behave like that in Monte or Nice, that much was certain. But most of those here tonight were quite presentable, a few quite pretty even. However this didn't apply to the one who was now crucifying 'I Will Survive'.

Blond regarded the singer more closely. She looked to be in her mid-forties but it was difficult to tell with the amount of slap she'd trowelled on her face. Five feet two, Blond's expert eye told him, five six in her heels. Long peroxided hair; a blonde with a brunette base. She was dressed in a red crop-top and red silk skin-tight hipsters, an outfit far too young for her years; she might have been described as mutton dressed as lamb but that would have been unfair on mutton. The outfit revealed a foot of bare midriff. Blond, a connoisseur of the female form, held the view that bare midriffs were fine as long as the women displaying them didn't carry so much as an ounce of surplus flesh. The incarnation of Gloria Gaynor now howling like a banshee into the microphone had about three stones of surplus flesh, a goodly portion of which had taken up residence between the bottom of her crop-top and the top of her hipsters. Blond visibly shuddered at the very sight of it.

> *I've got all my life to live*
> *I've got all my love to give*
> *And I'll survive*
> *I will survive*
> *I will survive....hey hey!*

The song ended and Gloria took a bow, to wild applause and shouts of appreciation. She made no move to leave the stage after the applause and cheers had dwindled. For one horrible moment Blond thought she was about to treat her audience to an encore, probably 'Here Come The Girls', but even if that had been the case he would have been saved from it by the next performer leaping onto the stage, snatching the microphone from her grasp and pushing her roughly out of the way, to friendly cheers and jeers from the crowd. No time was wasted at all, no ceremony stood upon, the show must go on, and the next performer was into his stride in the time it takes to say 'Evenin' everbody mah name is Elvis Presley', which is exactly what he did say, before starting to sing.

> Now since my baby left me
> I've found a new placed to dwell
> It's down at the end of Lonely Street
> At Heartbreak Hotel......

Blond reflected that if the performer on the stage made a habit of singing in the bath, or anywhere else within the confines of the house, that it was no small wonder his baby had left him, both sets of next-door neighbours too, for he was truly awful. Blond himself was the possessor of a passable baritone but even he would not have got up in public and sang, and especially not in white cowboy boots and a sequin-encrusted pink jumpsuit.

Looking around, as the murdering of 'Heartbreak Hotel' continued, Blond observed that apart from Elvis several others amongst the throng had taken the trouble to dress up as the person they were to impersonate that evening. Among them was a Dolly Parton look-alike with even bigger breasts than Dolly, who would probably soon be telling all the females in the room to 'Staynd By Their Men'; an Ozzy Osbourne complete with live bat; and an Elton John, although the last named could simply have been a bespectacled little bald man with two club feet who was merely a member of the audience.

Elvis was going down rather well, possibly because most of the audience were singing along with him and couldn't hear him, The King obviously being a particular favourite of theirs. Blond by now had had enough but was too much of a gentleman to leave whilst a singer was in mid-performance, even one as bad as the present incumbent of the stage. However the song soon mercifully

ended and Blond was about to go back down the passage
to his pork pie and another pint before returning to the
hotel and bed when he was stopped, just as surely and
abruptly as if he had walked into a brick wall, by the
sight of the next performer making her way up to the
stage.

She was a gigantic woman, six feet ten inches tall if she
was an inch and built, as they say in more genteel circles,
like a brick outhouse. (But in Stockport like a brick
shithouse.) She was attired in a heavily scuffed brown
leather gilet worn over a red and white lumberjack shirt,
jeans and hobnail boots. On her head she sported an
Australian bush hat completely encircled by about a
dozen dangling corks. Her hair, the colour and texture of
straw, stuck out from under the hat like fried bread. What
could be seen of her features through the curtain of corks
made Blond wish the hat had sported even more corks; a
burnished red face, little piggy china blue eyes, and a pug
nose more like a snout. Any doubts that despite her
appearance she was not a daughter of the Antipodes were
dispelled immediately she began to sing in the broadest
Australian accent Blond had ever heard, the diction of the
inhabitants of Ramsey Street being as correct a rendition
of the English language and as cultured as Joanna
Lumley's when compared to it.

> *When I was a gal*
> *And old Shep was a pup*
> *Over hills and meadows we'd stray*
> *Just a gal and her dog*
> *We were both full of fun*
> *We grew up together that way......*

The audience, having the good sense to have a healthy
distaste of either Australians or the song Old Shep,
probably both, soon began to pay her far less attention than
they had given the previous two performers, many of them

striking up conversations with their neighbours, a few others making their way to the bar to replenish their pint pots.

> As the years fast did roll
> Old Shep he grew old
> His eyes were fast growing dim
> And one day the doctor looked at me and said
> I can do no more for him......

The woman suddenly stopped singing. Then, glaring balefully at the audience, she bellowed at the top of her voice: "Quiet you pommie bastards, there's a fucking dog dying here!"

The buzz of conversation dropped immediately. Another baleful glance from the giant Australian, this one even more menacing than the previous one, stopped it completely.

"That's more like it," she said, and continued with the song. However the state of someone's next-door-neighbour's garden and the goings-on in Coronation Street on the telly the previous evening, along with other such absorbing topics, once again became more important to some members of the audience than the state of Old Shep's health, and before long the buzz of conversation was back to its previous level. The monstrosity on the stage stuck it for a moment or two then suddenly stopped singing again, glared ferociously at the audience and bellowed: "Shut... the... fuck... up!"

Most of the audience shutted the fuck up immediately, but a few were more lax. Not for much longer though as the Aussie, making as though to tear open the front of her shirt said: "Or have I to take my bra off?"

The effect of the words was electric. All conversation ceased immediately. Blond was quite amazed, not least because, as unwholesome a sight as the woman was, she did have one redeeming feature. A magnificent pair of breasts.

Large, full, round, and straining at the cotton of her lumberjack shirt like two melons in a sack. And yet apparently not one of the men present wanted to see them in the flesh.

Everyone in the room, every one, was now giving the Australian their undivided attention. She held their collective gaze for about ten seconds, then smiled and said: "Well then. Now let's have no bloody more of it," then continued with the song.

CHAPTER FIVE

FAÇADE

The following day found James Blond in the office of the Stockport Information Officer, Mr Medlock. His cover was that he was John Bland, an entrepreneur who was considering re-locating part of his rubber conglomerate to Stockport.

"Stockport has always been an important town. In pre-Roman days it was a strategic link across the River Mersey from the south into the north-west. Today it remains the nexus of a national and international communications network," Medlock said, for the third time in the last few minutes.

Medlock's speech on Stockport, which he recited quite regularly to school groups, local history enthusiasts and frequent visiting parties from Stockport's twin towns of Beziers in France and Heilbronn in Germany, took exactly fifteen minutes. The council official, a meticulous man to a fault, knew it was fifteen minutes because he had timed it as such, and on the occasions he'd checked he had been accurate to plus or minus ten seconds, an achievement in which he took no little pride. However today the speech had already taken fourteen minutes and he was still only five minutes into it, due to the fact that Blond had twice fallen asleep. On each occasion Medlock, unsure as to how much of his teach-in Blond had missed whilst he was dead to the world, and determined that his guest should get a complete as possible picture of Stockport, had started again from the beginning.

The reason why Blond was finding it difficult to stay awake was twofold; Medlock, as is often the case with people who have to deliver the same speech time after time, did it on automatic pilot. Furthermore he delivered it in one of the most monotonous voices Blond had ever had to listen to, it's lack of intonation having possibly sent more people to sleep than Horlicks. The secret agent would have bet that he was by no means the first recipient of Medlock's speech to have been driven into the arms of Morpheus.

The other reason Blond found it difficult to stay awake was that he'd had precious little sleep the night before. In his anxiety to get some food inside him he had relegated to the back of his mind the fact that although he liked pork pies as much as the next man pork pies did not like him, and invariably left him with heartburn and indigestion. He'd also had more to drink than was his intention.

His plan on returning to the bar after witnessing the karaoke had been to eat the pork pie and then retire for the evening, but the pie was even better than the landlord had promised and he ordered a second. Another pie being not much use without another pint he ordered another. Whilst he was drinking it the fearful racket from up the passageway thankfully came to a premature end when the karaoke machine broke down. It didn't stop the karaoke fans from singing however, but without the benefit of the music and loudspeakers the volume was much quieter, and because of this Blond decided that another couple or three pints of Robbie's, as everyone affectionately called the local brew, wouldn't do him any harm at all. But he had reckoned without the pork pies and the two pints he'd already had, and due to the heartburn and indigestion that the pies later induced in him he didn't manage to drop off to sleep until turned one-o-clock, and by a quarter past one he had woken up for a pee thanks to the five pints of Robbie's he'd consumed. To people fortunate enough not to be plagued with a prostate condition this wouldn't represent much of a problem; they would merely empty their bladder and quickly return to the Land of Nod, there to dwell sleeping soundly until morning. But people with a prostate problem do not discharge their five pints of liquid in one go; it's one pint at a time, and even then only if they're lucky, and if they're not it's more like half a pint. Blond was not lucky in this respect and had made eight trips to the bathroom before morning. The twin assault of sleep deprivation and the monotonous sound of Medlock's voice had done for him.

"In Stockport Viaduct the town of Stockport boasts one of the largest brick structures in Europe. It was built in 1840 to carry trains from Manchester to London across the River Mersey. Over 11 million bricks were used in the construction of its 27 arches," Medlock droned on. "Stockport is well provided for with sporting and recreational facilities with twenty one sports and activity centres with facilities for squash, badminton, basketball, weight training and many other minority sports. There are nine indoor swimming pools, over two hundred parks and playgrounds, many with facilities for tennis, putting, crown green bowling, soccer, cricket etc, two athletics tracks, eleven libraries, two museums and two historic houses, an art gallery, a civic theatre and fourteen golf courses."

Blond yawned as he felt sleep begin to claw him back into its darkness again. Manfully shrugging it off, and while Medlock paused for breath, he considered the less than riveting facts the council official had given him thus far. Taking every last one of them into consideration he could not come up with a single reason why someone would want to dominate Stockport. Dynamite it, yes; several reasons had put themselves forward as a sound case for blowing up the town, karaoke nights at the pub he'd been in the previous evening being at the forefront of them.

The absolute best thing Blond could say about Stockport was that it was commonplace. A common place in fact. It didn't have anything out of the ordinary that a hundred other large towns scattered throughout the land didn't have, and nothing they did have. The exception to this, the one thing Blond had noticed that had pretentions to class, and one couldn't help but notice it as it was hard by the M 60 motorway that bisected the centre of the town, was an enormous futuristic-looking pyramid-shaped building constructed almost entirely of blue tinted glass. Blond had taken the impressive looking Aztec-inspired structure to be an arts centre or perhaps a museum, a Cheshire Guggenheim maybe, but on enquiring he had been informed that it was nothing more glamorous than the offices of the Co-operative Bank. Stockport had blown its only chance.

"Local government in Stockport is stable and open," Medlock continued, "and has ambition and direction for the future. The local authority is committed to increasing public participation through a Citizens' Panel and a comprehensive public consultation strategy. It is determined to provide best value in public services. In 2002 and again in 2003 the Audit Commission rated the Council as 'good', the second from the top category. It is ever striving for excellence." He stopped and smiled at Blond. "Any questions, Mr Bland?"

Blond struggled to wakefulness. "Is that it? You've finished?"

"Unless you have any questions? Or unless you'd like me to go into more detail about the hundred and twenty neighbourhood recycling centres within the borough, with particular regard to the Schools Waste Action Clubs to educate the future generation, which is a particular interest of mine and of which I am something of an authority."

"No...no thank you," Blond said quickly. "Regretfully I must refuse. Absorbing though I'm sure it must be." He smiled. "So little time, so little time to do it."

"Anything else you would like to know then?" Medlock persisted, a dog loathe to give up its bone.

In fact Medlock's talk had not been totally without value to Blond. For buried amongst the statistics about Stockport's many parks and gardens and sports facilities had been the information that there were extensive underground air raid shelters and a labyrinth of passages cut into the soft, red sandstone under the town centre, a relic from the Second World War. Catacombs could very well be of interest to anyone planning to take over the town; as a nerve centre; a cache for explosives; an underground communications network.

There was also something else contained within the town's limits, much to Blond's surprise, that was of interest to him. A casino.

Blond, who had gambled with his life on countless occasions, was also not averse to a little gamble on the throw of a dice or the turn of a card now and again, and fully intended to make use of the casino that evening. The establishment was named Casino Royale, which registered with Blond as the title of the first of the James Bond books. If he had thought about it at all it would only have been to reach the conclusion that it must be one of many casinos named Casino Royale - the extracting of money from the pockets of their clients being a more obvious characteristic of casino owners than the dreaming up of imaginative and unique names for their enterprises.

Blond got to his feet. "No, I think that's all I need to know, thank you Mr Medlock," he said, but no sooner had he done so than he thought of something. "Unless….have you ever heard of a Dr Goldnojaws?"

Medlock smiled. "Oh indeed. I should think everyone in Stockport has heard of Dr Goldnojaws. Only recently that very gentleman donated one million pounds to Stockport Children's Charities."

Blond perked up immediately. This was more like it. "Really?"

"And not only that, he also…."

But Blond never did find out what Goldnojaws also did, leastwise not from Medlock, as at that moment the Information Officer's phone rang, and after taking the call he hurriedly excused himself, an important planning meeting that required his attendance had been brought forward and he had to leave immediately. Blond was unconcerned, he would find out everything he needed to know about Dr Goldnojaws soon enough. He had already learned that his adversary had made himself very popular with the town council by donating a large amount of money to local charities. This of course would ensure that his activities in the town wouldn't be looked at too closely, if at all, by the local authorities, and that any future plans he had would be viewed in a sympathetic light.

*

Back in his hotel room Blond, coffeeless, after having rung room service only to be informed by the ball-breaker of a receptionist that the chef had gone to a funeral, made plans for the rest of the day. Facilities for making coffee in the room were on hand in the shape of jars of Nescafe and Coffee Mate but both were empty, mate.

Blond's appointment with Dr Goldnojaws at Façade was for ten-o-clock the following morning so the first thing he had to do was discover the factory's location. For some reason it was in neither the local phone book nor the Yellow Pages. He also wanted a good look at Stockport in the daylight as what he'd seen of it thus far, apart from the short trip down the A6 from the Cheshire Towers to the Town Hall, had been in the dark. The town after all must have something going for it, he reasoned, something he'd perhaps missed, for someone to want to dominate it. Certainly whatever that something was had not become apparent from all that Medlock had told him about Stockport in painful detail a couple of hours ago.

He also wanted to take a look at the underground air raid shelter system to see for himself its extent, and to gauge its possibilities.

Finding Façade proved to be easy; calling at the first shoe shop he came across he struck gold immediately. The shoe shop owner purchased shoes from them on a regular basis, and very good shoes they were too apparently. The address was in the phone book, but under its previous name of Stockport Real Shoes, the concern having been re-named Façade only quite recently (when Goldnojaws took them over no doubt, surmised Blond). It was to be found in the Offerton area of Stockport near to the old and now defunct hat factory. Thanking the shoe shop owner for the information, and for the directions to Offerton with which she had kindly furnished him, Blond got back behind the wheel of the Lada and headed for Façade.

Red bricks it transpired were in no short supply in the town of Stockport, as apart from the 11 million used in the construction of the famous railway viaduct almost everything else seemed to be built from them, the rare stone building appearing as an oasis in a Sahara of red bricks. Façade, when he arrived outside it, was inevitably made of red bricks; as was the large chimney alongside it, a survivor both from an age gone by and from the late Fred Dibnah.

The two-storey factory, Blond assessed, was roughly sixty yards in length by thirty yards wide. It had originally been an old cotton mill judging by the architecture and the large windows. At the left-hand side was the entrance and a single-storied reception area. A sign above the entrance, in red joined-up writing, read 'Façade'.

And that was the sum total of what Blond learned from his visit. It might have been possible to glean more if he had looked through one of the ground floor windows to see what was going on inside, but only at the risk of attracting the attention of a passer-by, of which there were always several, the factory being located in a built-up area. Blond was not over-concerned, contenting himself with the knowledge that all he would probably see would be workers engaged in the manufacture of shoes, which was after all Goldnojaws' cover.

One detail about the building which Blond noted was that it was only possible to see in through some of the windows, maybe three-quarters of them; the rest of them, those farthest from the reception area, were painted over with black paint. To keep the sun out? Or prying eyes maybe?

Back behind the wheel of the Lada Blond drove the couple of miles to Stockport town centre, and ten minutes later parked up on the Merseyway car park that bestrides the shopping precinct with its ubiquitous chain stores. From there he made his way to the nearby Air Raid Shelters complex.

On arriving he was pleased to discover that they had guided tours. Excellent, it would make it much easier for him to find out what the air raid shelters were all about than it had been to discover any secrets the Façade factory might have. Blond bought his ticket at the kiosk and waited for the next tour to start, in ten minutes time a notice informed him. As he waited he took in an audio visual presentation that 'helped to provided firsthand experience of what life was liked in 1940's war-torn Britain', and very good it was too.

When the tour started Blond found the shelters, hacked out of red sandstone, to be even more extensive than he had imagined. The largest of them, the Chestergate Hotel as it was affectionately known, 'because it lay under the Chestergate area of the town', the guide had informed Blond's party, could accommodate five thousand people. He went on to further inform them that it had been fully equipped with electric lighting, plumbed-in toilets, bunks, benches, a first aid station and a canteen, many features of which still remained, and was apparently so comfortable that on hearing the all clear after an air raid many of the occupants didn't want to come out. In fact the complex was a veritable underground small town. And an absolutely ideal venue for a power base, Blond thought.

"Today, you can step back in time and experience the sights and sounds of Britain's Home Front as you wander around a core area of authentically reconstructed tunnels," said the guide, concluding the tour.

As they made their way back down the main tunnel to the start point Blond fell into conversation with the guide, a sprightly seventy-year-old who himself may very well have been one of those who had taken refuge in the shelters as a boy, when the Luftwaffe was doing its worst.

"So how long have you been doing this?" Blond asked.

The guide thought for a moment. "Oh, must be about ten years now. When I took early retirement. I wanted something to keep me active." Then he added, sadly, bitterly, "Shan't be active for much longer though."

"Oh?"

"Bastard Council is selling it off aren't they. Didn't you know? It was in all the papers. Yes, it's shutting down for good next week."

Blond commiserated. "Not paying I suppose. That's the reason most local authorities trot out these days."

"Money!" The guide spat out the word. "That's the reason all right. But not because it isn't paying; oh no, it's because somebody with more money than sense is buying it. Going to build a ten storey up market department store over the top of it and turn the shelters into the world's biggest Father Christmas's grotto, he says. Somebody name of....now what was it....silly sort of name....Gold....Gold something or other."

Blond's ears pricked. "Goldnojaws? Dr Goldnojaws?"

"That's him." The guide scowled. "That's the rotten sod."

Blond could see why Goldnojaws would want to get his hands on such a desirable place as the air raid shelter complex and it certainly wasn't for transforming it into a Santa's grotto.

By now they were back at the start point. "Well thank you very much," Blond said, taking out his wallet, withdrawing a crisp ten pound note and handing it to the guide. It cheered up the old man no end.

CHAPTER SIX

CASINO ROYALE

Blond checked his reflection in the full length mirror. Proud of his appearance, and ever mindful to maintain it, it was a ritual he followed religiously before setting out anywhere.

Blond was that rare being, a lady's man who was also a man's man. There was scarcely a woman in the land who would not have fallen for his blond good looks, quick mind and athletic physique, given half the chance; hardly a man who would not have been attracted by his élan and sense of adventure.

Blond hadn't packed his dinner jacket, it would be superfluous on this occasion, so the navy blue mohair would have to suffice. His red tie and white shirt set it off nicely, the ensemble, he noted as he made the slightest adjustment to the knot in his tie, giving him a distinctly patriotic look. And why not? He was nothing if not British, and to the core. Satisfied with his appearance, he turned from the mirror, fit and raring to go.

Whenever he spent an evening at a casino Blond liked to feel as relaxed as possible, it helped his game, and whenever practicable he would have a thorough full body massage prior to hitting the tables. The previous night he had noticed a sign in the foyer indicating that the hotel boasted a health spa, and had earlier phoned the receptionist. "Can I get a massage?" he had enquired.

"The chef's only just got back from a funeral," was the receptionist's unhelpful reply.

Chef? Obviously the woman had misheard him. "I said a massage, not a sausage," he said, then added tartly.

"Not that there would be much chance of my getting a sausage."

"The chef is a masseur," the receptionist replied. She passed on this information as though every chef in the world doubled as a masseur and that Blond must be some sort of imbecile not to be aware of it. After a slight pause and before Blond could frame a suitably cutting reply she went on. "Hold on a minute, he's here now." The line went silent for a moment. "He says give him five minutes and he'll be right up."

"An unusual combination," Blond observed soon afterwards, as the chef went to work on him, melting away the tensions built up over the day. "A masseur in addition to being a chef. Which came first?"

"The masseur part. I planned to have my own parlour once; strictly legit, nothing seedy. Then I got interested in cookery. I've Delia and Keith Floyd to thank for that. I just do it now to keep my hand in and make an extra bob or two on the side."

"You're very good," said Blond, meaning it. Certainly better at massaging than boiling eggs, if the four minute egg he had ordered at breakfast was anything to go by, Blond thought. If the chef's sense of timing had been applied to Roger Bannister's attempt to run the first sub four minute mile the athlete wouldn't have broken eight minutes let alone four.

"Thank you I'm sure. I did Georgie Best a couple of times." He reflected on this for a moment, and added, "Didn't do him much good though. In the end."

"No."

"Turn over would you."

Blond did as he was bidden. The chef went to work on his chest and arms.

"Here on business are you Mr Bland?"

"Yes."

"From the Smoke are you?"

Did people still call London the Smoke? Apparently in Stockport they did. "That's right."

"Arsenal, Chelsea?"

"Pardon?"

"Football. Or Spurs maybe?"

"Oh. No, I'm a rugger man; Harlequins when I can manage it; Wasps occasionally. I don't watch too much football."

"I wish I didn't." The chef said this with feeling but then bucked up immediately. "Mind you things could change, and soon; we're expecting big things at County now we've been taken over. Yes, apparently he's seriously minted this Dr Goldnojaws character, from what they say, and if the sky's his limit who knows? We could be up there with Man U one of these days."

Blond sat up. "Dr Goldnojaws? Someone named Dr Goldnojaws has bought your football club?"

"Lock stock and barrel. The works."

"How very interesting."

"How's that?"

"I mean for you; and the town's football supporters," the secret agent added quickly, anxious that the chef shouldn't suspect it was Goldnojaws himself who was of interest to him. One couldn't be too careful, people talk.

The rest of the massage took place in near silence, the chef making a couple of attempts at further conversation but remaining silent once Blond had made it apparent he didn't wish to talk any further.

He needed to think about why Dr Goldnojaws would want to add the town's football club to his holdings.

*

Now feeling cool and comfortable after a refreshing cold shower following the massage Blond drove to the casino. It was a brick building of course, what else in Stockport. It was completely undistinguished and could have been a bakery or a branch library or something similar, and probably was in a previous incarnation, had it not been for the large neon 'Casino Royale' lettering on the façade. Line drawings of dice, cards, chips and cocktail glasses in various hues completed the garish sign.

The tuxedoed bouncer stationed at the door was an unsavoury-looking slaphead with a broken nose and designer stubble. On some men designer stubble looks good - Blond had carried it off easily the few times he had chosen to wear it - but on others it just looks as though they haven't bothered to shave. In the case of the Casino Royale bouncer it was definitely the latter.

As Blond passed through the entrance to the casino the bouncer gave him only the most cursory of glances, riff-raff being his quarry, not well set up men in expensive-looking suits. Blond took little notice of him, just enough to reflect that the man couldn't be much of a bouncer if he had a broken nose; good bouncers hand out broken noses rather than become the recipient of them.

Inside the building Blond learned that the gaming part of the casino comprised a single, very large, room. The time was ten-o'clock, early doors for a casino, and the scent and smoke and sweat, the baggage a casino inevitably brings with it, hadn't yet had time to fully pollute the atmosphere. The usual games of chance were on offer; slot machines, roulette, blackjack, stud poker, baccarat. The place was by no means crowded but there was action at most of the tables and five or six people were feeding the slots in the bored manner that such slaves to these machines employ.

Blond had always been a gambler. Although he enjoyed all the card games and played them expertly his preferred game of chance was roulette. He liked the simplicity of it. There was none of the protracted business of drawing one card at a time, prolonging the agony, as is the case with card games, but one simple bet in which you either won or you lost, depending to a large extent on your luck. A true game of chance.

After visiting the bar, where he bought a large gin and tonic, his usual drink of choice whilst gambling, Blond went to the cuisse and changed two hundred pounds into ten pound chips. Not a lot, but he could always buy more later if required. It usually wasn't. Armed now with alcoholic refreshment and the means with which to bet, all that a man about town requires for a pleasant evening's gaming, he made for one of the two roulette wheels.

When playing the wheel Blond had a complicated system of his own involving first and last dozens, which he now commenced to put into operation. He played steadily for fifteen minutes at the end of which he was down to the tune of eighty pounds. A mere bagatelle for a man of Blond's means and it was still early days; one had to bring patience to the table in addition to money when using a system.

The only other people at the table were a couple whom Blond judged to be in their late forties, he with an ill-fitting red toupee, she wearing far too much rouge. They weren't at the moment playing the wheel, the single pile of fifty pound chips in front of them lying untouched. Nor did they seem to have any awareness of Blond, contenting themselves with watching the ball spin round the roulette wheel and taking careful note of where it eventually came to rest. Finally Toupee spoke. "Now. Put the lot on red."

Too Much Rouge bridled. "All five hundred pounds?"

"The lot." Toupee was adamant. "As we agreed. I'm fed up with this pissing about every week, losing a bit here and a bit there until we've blown the lot. Get it all on at one go I say, get it over with, muck or nettles."

"Well all right then," said Too Much Rouge, but sounding unconvinced she would be doing the right thing.

"On red. It's landed on black the last eight times; it's bound to land on red this time."

Too Much Rouge demurred. "Not necessarily. There's just as much chance it will land on black again."

"What?" Utter disbelief was written on Toupee's face. "Don't talk daft, woman. What planet are you from?"

Too Much Rouge stuck to her guns. "Well there is."

"Don't talk so fucking stupid." Toupee turned to Blond. "Tell her she's talking fucking stupid."

Although he had become interested in the altercation Blond had no wish to get embroiled in a domestic. However he was disinclined to let the matter pass without comment, especially as Toupee had asked him for his opinion, more or less. Apart from that a lady had been insulted and therefore a gallant stance was called for. "Actually the lady is correct," he said, smoothly and with authority.

Toupee's eyes almost popped out. "What?"

Blond enlarged. "Even if the ball were to land on black ten times, or even a hundred times, the chances of it falling on black the next time are even."

"A hundred times?"

"A million times come to that."

"See, Clever Clogs" said Too Much Rouge, with a disparaging look at Toupee.

"Bollocks," said Toupee. "The man's talking absolute bollocks. Now do as you're told and put the money on red; it must have more chance, law of averages."

Too Much Rouge remained unconvinced. "My instincts are telling me to put it on black."

"And your husband is telling you to put it on fucking red, so put it on fucking red," fumed Toupee. "That's five hundred quid. How many fish have I had to flog to make that? How many stinking mackerel have I had to gut and fillet and plaice to bone for five hundred quid? Do as you're told and put it on red."

Too Much Rouge indicated Blond. "But this gentleman says...."

"I don't give a flying fuck what this gentleman says, put it on red or I'll fucking choke you!"

"Place your bets please," said the croupier.

Too Much Rouge slid the pile of chips onto the nearest red square. The croupier gave the wheel a spin. The ball careened around. Then, just as the wheel was about to stop, and with a defiant look at Toupee, Too Much Rouge slid the chips onto a black square. The wheel came to rest.

"Red thirty two," cried the croupier

Only when Blond had convinced himself that Toupee was not immediately going to carry out his threat to strangle Too Much Rouge – though the secret agent was of course quite aware he could do nothing to prevent the intended offence taking place once he had departed the scene – did he leave the roulette wheel, having decided that a change of game might bring with it a change of luck. A few hands of stud maybe? He made for one of the four tables offering that form of poker.

Blond had noticed the girl when he was at the roulette wheel. From sixty feet away she had looked pretty. Now, as he took a seat at her table, he could see he had been wrong. Hopelessly wrong. She was beautiful. One of the most beautiful women he had ever seen. Her hair was jet black; lustrous, soft hair, which she wore long, framing her face. Her eyes, set wide apart, as is often the case with extreme beauty, were a deep violet colour. Although she was employed in a casino her skin didn't have the pallor associated with people who worked through the night and slept through the day, but was lightly tanned and glowing with health. Her face bore little trace of make-up; it had no need of it, just the slightest touch of lipstick on her wide, sensual mouth. She was wearing a simple black dress, temptingly tight across her full breasts. Round her neck was a thin gold chain, a letter 'D' hanging from it. Danielle? Dolores? Darling, certainly. She glanced at Blond as he took his seat. Her smile was warm and welcoming.

"Shall I deal you in, sir?"

Blond nodded. "Please."

The girl's perfectly manicured fingers expertly shuffled the cards then dealt them to Blond and the four other players seated around the table.

Blond played steadily for twenty minutes or so. He was normally quite adept at stud but on this occasion found it difficult to concentrate, the beautiful croupier being a distraction he could barely take his eyes off. After dropping a hundred pounds he was about to cut his losses and head back to the roulette wheel when the girl pushed her chair back, got to her feet and a male croupier took her place. Blond watched her depart. Impossibly, the view of her from the back was better than it had been from the front. Her derriere was not like that of most women, a bottom sat atop a pair of legs, but an extension of her legs; pert, rounded, firm, the thin material of her dress stretched even more tightly over it than the material that spanned her breasts. A bottom to die for. A bottom to live for.

She headed for the entrance and disappeared outside. A minute later Blond pocketed his remaining chips and followed her.

The girl hadn't gone very far. Blond found her standing at the top of the steps leading to the entrance to Casino Royale. She noticed him as he stepped outside. She smiled that warm welcoming smile again and indicated the cigarette she was smoking. "Bacca time," she explained.

Blond returned her smile and took out a silver cigarette case. "Do you mind if I join you?"

"Be my guest."

Blond opened the cigarette case and offered it to the girl. "Would you like to try one of mine? I have them especially made for me by Du Frais of Mayfair."

The girl looked at the cigarettes with their distinctive double silver band. "Maybe later."

Maybe later? Was that a promise of things to come? Later when? Later back in the casino or later back at her place? He looked at her but her expression told him nothing. But she hadn't said maybe later for nothing. He wasted no time in finding out. "My name is James Blond. And you are?"

"Divine Bottom."

Blond savoured the name, rolled it round his tongue. "Divine Bottom. What a wonderfully appropriate name."

She smiled that captivating smile once more. "It's not my real name. My real name is...."

Blond held up a cautionary hand, stopping her. "No. Don't tell me, let me guess." He thought for a moment.

With a name like Divine Bottom she must obviously have previously had a plain Christian name. He took a guess. "Jane Bottom? Mary Bottom? Sally....?"

"No," she laughed, "You're on the wrong track altogether. The Divine part of my name is quite genuine. It's the bottom that's false. I've got a false bottom." She giggled, informing Blond that along with her beauty she also had a beguiling sense of humour. Good. He enjoyed making love to women who knew how to laugh. Just as long as they weren't fat or plain.

"So your real surname is?"

"Shufflebottom. I dropped the Shuffle and now I'm just Bottom."

Now it was Blond's turn to be amusing. "When it comes to aptness, and given your dexterity with playing cards, you might just as well have dropped the Bottom and kept the Shuffle, making you Divine Shuffle; a wonderful name for a croupier."

She laughed, enjoying him. "Right. I never thought of that."

He looked directly into her eyes. "So, Divine Bottom, how long have you worked at the Casino Royale?"

She thought for a moment. "Er....two weeks tomorrow."

Blond was surprised. "You must have worked as a croupier at some other place?"

"Yes, but mostly here."

Blond shook his head. "I refuse to believe that. Judging by the dextrous way you handle cards you must have...." The mischievous look in her bewitching violet eyes stopped him.

"Just teasing," she smiled. "I've worked here for close to four years in all. But until two weeks ago this place was called the Gala Casino. When he new owner Dr Goldnojaws took it over he changed the name to Casino Royale."

Blond blinked. Dr Goldnojaws? Again? His mind raced. The Air Raid Shelters. Stockport County Football Club. Now the Casino Royale, all bought by Goldnojaws? What the devil was the man up to? The significance of Goldnojaws naming the casino after the first of the Bond books, Casino Royale, was not lost on Blond either. Goldnojaws playing his little name games again?

"You know him?" Divine said, on seeing his reaction.

Her question halted his further speculations. "No. No it's just that it's such an unusual name," he white lied.

"I suppose. With a name like Divine Bottom unusual names sometimes pass me by."

"I don't suppose he's here tonight?" Blond would have liked a sneak preview of his latest adversary and if there was any chance of it he meant to take it. He was to be disappointed though.

"No. At least I don't think so, but to tell you the truth I wouldn't know him from Adam. He's something of a mystery man from what I've heard. Doesn't go out much, keeps himself to himself." She finished her cigarette and tossed the butt into a convenient pot plant. "Well, duty calls." She glanced at the watch on her slim wrist. "Just an hour to go and I'm done. I finish at twelve, I'm on earlies this week thank God."

"And when you've finished?"

"Home to Didsbury, and supper." The pause was for only a moment. "You're welcome to join me if you haven't already eaten?"

While Blond waited for Divine to finish her shift he filled in the time at the baccarat table. When it was time to leave he had slightly cut his losses for the evening to a hundred and thirty pounds. Unfortunate, but he would happily have lost a hundred and thirty pounds on every occasion he spent time at the gaming tables so long as there was the slightest chance of it throwing up an opportunity to get into Divine Bottom's knickers.

During the three mile drive to Didsbury in Divine's new Mini Cooper – Blond quite naturally not wishing to destroy the aura that surrounded his persona by admitting that he drove a Lada – he found out a little about Divine. She was aged twenty three, had left school when she was eighteen with a university place to go to, but her gap year had turned into a gap five years when in a visit to Las Vegas she had become completely captivated by the gambling scene. She had taken a job in a casino for a while, had become a croupier, and had remained a croupier to this day. She might eventually go to university but she doubted it, she was earning good money at Casino Royale and she enjoyed the life. She was born and bred in Didsbury but had by now moved out of the family home and had a place of her own. She played tennis, liked to travel, and enjoyed every sort of music except rap and country & western.

Didsbury village is a suburb of Manchester, a dormitory for the students and teaching staff of the nearby Manchester University, its multicultured and multicoloured population making it cosmopolitan to Stockport's Cosmo Smallpiece. Divine's flat was just off Kingsway, the arterial road leading to Manchester's famous 'Curry Mile', thence on to the heart of the city centre some five miles away. The flat was small, but not too small, and comfortably, tastefully, furnished.

"Let's go through to the kitchen, we can talk while I fix us something to eat," said Divine, as they entered the flat. "But first let me get you a drink. I'm having a G and T."

"Make that two."

She mixed large gin and tonics for the pair of them and they took them into the small but well-equipped kitchen.

"What would you prefer? A sandwich? Or I have some quiche left I think." She made for the fridge.

"Perhaps a little er....cold, quiche." Blond was still feeling the chill of the early morning air from the short walk from Divine's parking spot to her flat. "I'm a little cold, actually."

Divine was at once concerned, protective. "Then what you need is something hot inside you."

"As the bishop said to the actress," smiled Blond, neatly reversing the scriptwriter provided witticism that Postlethwaite had used a couple of days ago.

She laughed easily, not in the least uncomfortable with the crude innuendo. She had heard far worse during her time at Casino Royale. "Pasta then, perhaps?" she asked. "Or I do a mean omelette?"

"An omelette I think. I enjoy pasta but I find it can lie a little heavy on the stomach... when making love is also on the menu." He took her in his arms as he said this. She melted into them at once. "You will make love with me tonight, will you, Divine?"

"I'd love to, James," she whispered, huskily. Blond's heart leapt. Testosterone rushed to his loins as though a tap had been opened. "But unfortunately I'm having my period."

Blond's heart leapt back faster than the proverbial off a shovel and the unrequired testosterone rushed back from whence it came. Recalling the debacle with Pisa Vass and not wishing to go through all that again he simply let go of Divine Bottom and walked out of her flat and her life forever.

CHAPTER SEVEN

DR GOLDNOJAWS

When Blond arrived for his appointment with Dr Goldnojaws he still hadn't fully recovered from the traumatic experience of the previous night. To have his advances rejected once, although on understandable grounds, was a blow. To be knocked back twice was a disaster.

He had brooded for most of the night on the matter but couldn't for the very life of him make any sense of what had happened last night with Divine Bottom and two weeks previously with Pisa Vass. It was only when he applied the same analytical methods to the task that he applied to his job as a secret agent that he began to see daylight.

First Blond had asked himself how many beautiful women he had made love to during his years with MI6. An educated guess told him the figure was six hundred, or as near to that figure as made no difference. Then, thanks to a telephone call to Maddox's secretary Miss Twopence, he had determined how many days per month the average woman of child-bearing age spent having her period. She had reported that it was five. Thankfully she hadn't asked him why he wanted this information, which saved Blond from having to spin her the cock-and-bull story he'd dreamed up about the Russians' plan to harness the power of pre-menstrual tension and put it to use to manufacture nuclear weapons, which in truth he had felt seemed a tad far-fetched, even for the Russians. Dividing the number of days in a month by five gave the answer one sixth, more-or-less, and dividing one sixth into the six hundred women he had slept with over the years produced a figure of one hundred. Therefore by the law of averages one hundred of the six hundred women should have been having their period when he had propositioned them.

And yet the actual figure was none. None whatsoever. Once Blond had seen it in this light he realised how very fortunate he had been in the past and his mood improved considerably. After all, he consoled himself, why should he be any more entitled to period-free women than the next man? He was the same as other men in most other instances; he ate as often as other men; he slept as often as other men; he went to the lavatory as often as other men. Check, he went to the lavatory more than other men since he'd developed the damned prostate gland problem that constantly plagued him nowadays.

Now, waiting for Goldnojaws to see him, he filled in the time by going over his cover story again. Nothing had been left to chance but SA-Seven was punctilious to a fault in his preparation; it was one of the attributes that made him the department's top agent.

His story was that he was John Bland, a sales director with L for Leather – a genuine business, should Goldnojaws choose to check up on it – a leather importing and manufacturing company based in Ealing, West London.

Before he left for Stockport Blond had been given a crash course in the basics of the shoe leather industry by the people at L for Leather and now knew enough about it to get by should Goldnojaws come up with any technical queries. If the worse came to the worst, and Goldnojaws were to ask something to which he didn't know the answer, he would say that his post was principally as a figurehead and that his staff could supply Goldnojaws with any information he may require. The bait, the reason why Goldnojaws had given Blond the time of day rather than leave the business to one of his minions, was a hundred thousand pounds worth of premium quality shoe leather for the knockdown price of fifty thousand pounds. The Department would square the difference with L for Leather. The reason given to Goldnojaws for the company's largesse was a slight over-production which had created a cash flow problem. The owner of Façade had fallen for the ploy, hook, line and sinker. Goldnojaws' plan may well have been to dominate Stockport but greed rarely fails to get a grip on man when a bargain is dangled in front of him.

Goldnojaws had been informed of Blond's arrival but it was now ten minutes past ten-o-clock. As there was still no sign from his secretary that her boss was ready to meet with him Blond got up to stretch his legs. And also to take another look at the shop floor, which he had already given a quick once-over on arriving at Façade.

The mezzanine outer office at Façade overlooked the workshop and Blond now took in for a second time the factory floor set out beneath him. If Façade was indeed a front he needed to know what it was a front for. But from what he could see from his vantage point it was to all intents and purposes what it was supposed to be; a factory engaged in the manufacture of shoes.

Blond observed once again that there was little in the way of large, sophisticated machinery. He had commented on this to Goldnojaws' secretary, who informed him that the company made only top of the range bespoke shoes, largely by hand and by traditional methods. They were completely organic. This was borne out by what Blond now observed as he looked down into the workshop; rows and rows of tables, a leather-aproned worker seated at each one, fashioning leather into shoes. Less like a factory, more like a giant cobbler's shop. The rest of the space was taken up by large piles of sheets of leather in various sizes, thicknesses and colours, and here and there pallets containing boxes, some empty, some of completed footwear.

It was whilst he was following the progress of one such pallet, steered by a worker in brown bib-and-brace overalls towards a set of large rubber double doors, that Blond saw the man in the white lab coat. On spotting him he caught his breath. He had seen him before somewhere, he was certain. But where?

Blond never forgot a face. It was another of the reasons he was so good at his job. He sometimes failed to put a name to the face immediately, and where and when and in what context he had seen it, but with due diligence it invariably came to him, and usually sooner rather than later. He now put the face through the rogues gallery of faces on permanent exhibition in his head. He soon located it, in the Russian section, between the lovely but deadly Miss Tractor Factory 1989 and the nymphomaniac Rosa Lott – lucky chap, smiled Blond to himself, I wouldn't mind being between those two myself – but he couldn't for the moment recall which name attached to it.

The man had passed through one of the doors into the main workshop. He had then walked a few paces forward, stopped as if in thought, then, as though he had forgotten something, turned and gone back through the door. Blond hoped he would return more or less immediately so he could get a better look at him, which might further jog his memory, but just then the receptionist called: "Dr Goldnojaws will see you now, Mr Bland."

The secretary opened the door to Goldnojaws' office, stood aside and Blond stepped in. Dr Goldnojaws got up from his seat and walked round his desk to welcome his visitor. "Come in, Mr Bland," he said. "Take a seat, please do."

Because it could possibly mislead him Blond made it a habit never to make a mental picture of someone before he met them for the first time. He knew from experience that it would turn out to be anything but an accurate representation, quite the reverse often being the case. Names invariably offered false clues and only served to point one in the wrong direction; how many people named Little were diminutive when the evidence presented itself? They were just as likely to be large. How many people called Stout turned out to be thin as a lath? If a person's name gave a clue as to what they looked like in the flesh then from his knowledge of the James Bond films Blond could reasonably have expected Dr Goldnojaws to be about seven feet tall with red hair, a mouthful of sharp metal teeth and a gadget on his right hand that could crack nuts, both the ones you get in shells and human ones; a fanciful figure to say the very least.

In the event, if Goldnojaws had turned out to match the above description Blond would have been less surprised than he was on seeing the figure now standing at the side of his desk inviting him to sit down. For Dr Goldnojaws was a dwarf. Not a midget, not an unusually small person whose limbs and features are of normal proportions, but a true dwarf, an abnormally small person with very short limbs and a head and body of near normal size. Blond would far rather his adversary had been about seven feet tall with red hair, a mouthful of sharp metal teeth and a gadget on his right hand that could crack nuts; far from Goldnojaws' size making him less of a threat Blond knew from past experience that it would make him even more of a threat. He was aware that history is littered with crazed degenerates of small stature; Adolf Hitler, Napoleon, Geronimo, at least two homosexual TV chat show hosts.

Dr Goldnojaws was dressed in a sober charcoal grey business suit, pale pink shirt and striped tie, and despite his size looked the typical businessman. His features were dark and swarthy, almost gipsy-like, and Blond immediately recognised a keen intelligence in his dark brown, almost black eyes. This was not Dopey or Sleepy he would be dealing with here, nor any of their five brothers.

Goldnojaws appearance had stopped Blond in his tracks. The secret agent now looked the dwarf up and down, which given his size only took a second and a minimum of eye movement, but enough for Goldnojaws to spot it.

"Two feet ten."

Blond blinked. "Pardon?"

"My height, Mr Bland. Two feet ten."

"I wasn't...." Blond started, but Goldnojaws held up a dismissive hand as though to save Blond the bother of lying or apologising. "Please. It is nothing with which to concern yourself, Mr Bland. I am in no way offended, I am quite used to it by now." He indicated the chair opposite his desk. "Please."

Blond did as he was bidden. Goldnojaws returned to his seat, took time to compose himself, then leaned forward and looked to his left and right conspirationally as though looking for possible eavesdroppers before taking Blond into his confidence, then said: "Let me tell you about being a dwarf, Mr Bland. In particular let me tell you about what I most dread." He looked keenly at the secret agent. "What do you suppose that might be?"

Blond could think of several things a dwarf might dread; being rejected by women; being looked down on by his fellow men just because of his size; literally being looked down on by ten-year-olds; trying to get a drink at a bar when he was the only man in the pub and the barman was deaf. But Blond was there to listen, to find things out, he wanted Goldnojaws to do the talking, not himself, because when people talk they sometimes talk too much and give things away, which they don't do by listening, so he said: "I really have no idea Dr Goldnojaws."

"It is being picked up, Mr Bland, as though I were a child." He paused for a moment before carrying on. "Can you imagine how utterly, utterly humiliating that must be for me? To have someone actually pick me up? It happened to me once. I had disembarked from an airplane and had to board a bus to Arrivals. It was a single high step up from the tarmac to the floor of the bus, maybe a foot. I could have coped with the situation with ease. I have dealt with similar situations many times in the past. The technique is to sit down on the step and lift up your legs before swivelling your body round on your bottom, then getting to your feet. Simple, if a trifle inelegant. But on this occasion

I wasn't given the chance to do that. Before I knew what was happening, before I could protest, the man behind me picked me up and popped me down on the bus. Then he patted me on the head and said 'There you go, little man.'" He paused for effect. "Little man! Can you imagine how I felt at that moment? The embarrassment?"

To his credit Blond felt genuinely sorry for Dr Goldnojaws. But only for a moment. That was all it took to remind himself that he was dealing here with a man who had set his heart on dominating Stockport. He said: "You have my deepest sympathy, Dr Goldnojaws. It must have been truly awful for you."

"Indeed. It was almost as bad as when I realised I would never be able to achieve my ambition." The inflexion of Goldnojaws' voice invited a response. Anxious for Goldnojaws to carry on holding court, Blond obliged. "And that was?"

"To be a policeman."

Only great resolve and even greater balance kept Blond from falling off his chair. An even greater show of resolve was needed to keep a straight face, as Goldnojaws continued. "As a boy it was the only thing I ever truly wanted. But it was not to be. Denied to me by an accident of birth, by a quirk of nature, bad luck, call it what you will." His face took on a sudden intensity. "I would have made a very good policeman too, Mr Bland. A top policeman. I could have been Goldnojaws of the Yard."

Blond very much doubted this as Goldnojaws wasn't even a yard of Goldnojaws, but refrained from pointing this out. Instead he said: "I'm sure you could Dr Goldnojaws." The explanation of the dwarf's lust for power was now becoming clearer to Blond. It was similar to the poacher turned gamekeeper syndrome except that in this case the roles were reversed, it was gamekeeper turned poacher; rejected by the police he had joined the ranks of the other side and become a criminal.

Goldnojaws was about to continue when his phone rang. He picked it up, listened for a moment or two, then started to give a list of instructions in a brisk, commanding voice. Before replacing the phone he turned to Blond. "Coffee, Mr Bland?"

"Please. Black, no sugar."

Goldnojaws spoke into the phone. "Have BloJob serve us coffee."

Whilst Goldnojaws had been speaking on the phone Blond had taken stock of his office. The wall behind the dwarf's desk was dominated by two five feet by five feet blown-up photographs of two different insects. Blond thought he recognised one of them as a crane fly whilst the other was possibly a grasshopper. As Goldnojaws replaced the phone he noted Blond's interest in the insects. "Do you like the photographs of my little friends, Mr Bland?" he said, swivelling round in his chair to look at them along with Blond. "The one on the left is a crane fly. Known familiarly as a Daddy Long Legs I believe. An insect of the family Tipulidae, order Diptera. A slender, mosquito-like body and extremely long legs, usually found around water or abundant vegetation. The one on the right is a locust, a species of short-horned grasshopper of the Orthopteran family, Acrididae. They often increase greatly in number and migrate long distances in destructive swarms." He turned to face Blond. "I take a keen interest in insects, Mr Bland. Particularly so in the case of crane flies and locusts, which are my especial favourites."

"Which is abundantly obvious from your impressive knowledge of them," said Blond, who could be as obsequious as the best of them when the occasion demanded.

It was then that Blond was surprised for the second time since entering Goldnojaws' office, when the door suddenly opened and the gigantic Australian woman from the pub karaoke the other night came in, bearing a tray.

"This is my factotum, BloJob," announced Goldnojaws, indicating her with an arm. "BloJob this is Mr Bland."

BloJob smiled at Blond through the curtain of dangling corks. It was not a friendly smile. It was a smile of utter malevolence. The woman was dressed exactly as she had been at the karaoke but her appearance was now made even more grotesque by her chomping continuously and open-mouthed on a wad of chewing gum, the effect being as a load of concrete circulating in a cement mixer, and almost as noisy. She now loped over to Goldnojaws' desk like some antipodean version of the Yeti and put down the tray.

"That will be all, BloJob." The factotum started to leave, however Goldnojaws had an afterthought. "Oh BloJob?"

BloJob turned. "Yeh?"

"Did you get the flags?"

BloJob pulled a face. "Aw shit."

Goldnojaws glared at her. "You didn't?"

"Forgot the little bastards, didn't I, Goldie." She shrugged an apology.

The dwarf lost his temper. "The flags are for my map you dumb Australian bitch!" As he said this he waved an arm in the direction of the huge map of Stockport which completely covered one wall of the office. Stuck in the map at various points were little flags, seven in all, Blond noted.

"I'll get 'em right now, Goldie, just you leave it to little ol' BloJob."

"And see that you do! It is vital I keep my map up to date."

Goldnojaws waited until BloJob had left the room then shaking his head sadly he turned to Blond. "Willing but no brain at all. An Australian of course. An ex-lover of mine; I took pity on her, found her a job when I'd had my fill of her body." Goldnojaws noticed Blond's look of surprise at the dwarf's pronouncement. "You are shocked that a man as diminutive as me would wish to take a lover so large, Mr Bland? The reason is quite simple. I like big women. When making love, unlike in matters of business, I like to be dominated."

If by dominated Goldnojaws meant woman on top Blond conjectured that with BloJob astride him Goldnojaws, as well as being dominated, stood an excellent chance of being laminated. Obviously this hadn't happened, so maybe he meant something else; whips, bondage perhaps; powerful men were well known for their unusual sexual predilections.

Goldnojaws broke into Blond's train of thought. "Shall we get down to business then, Mr Bland?"

"Of course." Blond stooped to open his briefcase.

"You have a bargain for me I believe?"

"Quite so. Allow me to show you a sample of what you can expect for your fifty thousand pounds, Dr Goldnojaws."

Goldnojaws dismissed Blond's suggestion with a wave of his arm. "That won't be necessary. My technical people will check out your sample and if it is of the quality you say it is then we can do business."

"I'm sure they will find it to be of excellent quality."

"Then we will have a deal. But now to more important matters. Do you bowl, Mr Bland?"

"Bowl?"

Goldnojaws nodded.

"Well I bowled a decent off break at school, but that was years...."

"No, not that sort of bowling," Goldnojaws interjected. He came round his desk and mimed the delivery action of a man playing bowls. "Crown green bowls."

"Ah."

"Do you play?"

Blond had played lawn, or flat green bowls; his father was an enthusiast and had roped him in for a game on several occasions. Good at most sports, he had soon picked up the game. "Not the crown green version I'm afraid," he said. "Although I have played flat green on occasion."

"The crown green game is a little different, but the important thing is the bowling action, which you will already have mastered. I therefore challenge you to a game tomorrow. What do you say?"

"But of course, Dr Goldnojaws." Blond suspected that the dwarf would probably beat him, but he was not about to turn the offer down; the more time he spent with Goldnojaws the more he was likely to discover what he was up to.

"With a wager of....say, a thousand pounds, to make it interesting." Blond hesitated momentarily. Goldnojaws noted this and said, his voice gently mocking, "Come come, Mr Bland, a thousand pounds must mean nothing to you, your commission from our little bit of business alone must amount to more than that."

In fact the reason for Blond's hesitance was that he didn't want to appear to be too eager. The Department would pick up the tab should he lose the game so losing the money didn't enter into the equation. But he didn't want Goldnojaws to think that. So after a moment or two more of supposed thinking about it he said, with a touch of reluctance: "Well, all right then, Dr Goldnojaws."

"Excellent."

Blond got to his feet. "Until tomorrow then."

"We will meet at the bowling green at Torkington Park. My secretary will give you directions. Four p.m. Prompt."

CHAPTER EIGHT

BLOND IS GIVEN A LESSON

Blond, requiring a set of bowls for his coming match with Goldnojaws, was fortunate that the town of Stockport is something of a stronghold of the sport and boasts one of crown green bowls' leading retail outlets, Premier Bowls. When he arrived there shortly after leaving Façade the helpful assistant Glyn informed Blond that although wooden *lignum vitae* bowls were still used by a few diehards, plastic was the modern bowl of choice, and that of the six main manufacturers of plastic bowls three were judged to be outstanding; Thomas Taylor, Drake's Pride and Henselite. Of the three Thomas Taylor shaded it in popularity with the bowling fraternity. Taking the assistant's advice Blond purchased a set of two pounds twelve ounces Taylor De-Luxe.

Five minutes later, armed with the shiny new bowls and a bowling bag along with a booklet on the rules of crown green bowls which the assistant had kindly thrown in, Blond was driving the Lada in the direction of St Thomas's Park. On questioning the assistant on the subject of bowling greens it had transpired that Stockport was almost as well served with them, both private and public, as it was with red bricks. Blond had further been advised that he would be better off making for one of the town's park greens rather than the green of a private club such as the Victoria or Houldsworth WMC clubs. "They only charge a quid and only then if the park warden calls round while you're playing, and he's got eighteen greens to cover so you'll probably get away without paying."

Blond was anxious to get in some practice before his game the following day with Dr Goldnojaws. He had no way of knowing how good the dwarf was at the sport but suspected he must be at the very least proficient, otherwise he wouldn't have thrown out the challenge.

Blond accepted that he would have to be better than Goldnojaws if he were to win. Not only better but much better. Because he knew instinctively, from the moment the gauntlet had been thrown down, that Goldnojaws would cheat. He saw it coming from a mile away, the parallels were too obvious to ignore; it would be James Bond's famous game of golf with Goldfinger all over again; a match in which Goldfinger had used every trick in the book, plus a few that weren't, in his attempts to defeat Bond. As all fans of the Bond books and movies are well aware Goldfinger's trickery and gamesmanship had failed. Blond was determined that where Goldfinger had failed to best James Bond so too would Goldnojaws fail to best James Blond.

Although Blond had never played crown green bowls before he was an accomplished player of the game of golf, and as such was wise to the devious ways some opponents are apt to resort to in order to obtain an unfair advantage; improving the lie of the ball, claiming a found ball was their lost ball when it was no such thing, claiming to have taken only five strokes at a hole when in reality they had taken six or seven; the ways of cheating during a game of golf are as diverse as they are legion.

Judging from what Blond had gleaned from a brief perusal of the booklet he had been given it appeared on the face of it that the sport of crown green bowls was a much more difficult game at which to cheat. There were no lost balls to look for and be magically 'found', one's lie couldn't be improved, and the score, in match conditions, was kept by a third party, known as a marker. Even the measuring of the bowls, when necessary, in order to determine which lay closest to the jack, was a task left to third parties; so no jiggery-pokery could take place there either.

There would be ways though, Blond was sure, and he was even surer that Goldnojaws would use those ways against him. He would need to be on his guard even more than usual.

Blond arrived at the St Thomas's green at the same time as three other men intent on a game of bowls. On noticing Blond one of them approached and asked him if he'd like to make them up in a game of doubles, their mate Chris having cried off due to a sick pigeon. Blond, knowing only the rudiments of the game, jumped at the chance to pick up a few tips from more experienced players. It would also give him the opportunity to quiz them on any possible cheating that might take place during a game. Even so, he felt duty bound to point out his lack of experience, and this he did. However it was not seen as a problem by his new friends, one of whom told Blond that he had two bowls just like anybody else and it was up to him to use them. A couple of minutes later the game was underway. Blond partnered Nigel Waddington, their opponents were Ivor Fantam and Peter Hulme.

Blond wasn't much use to Nigel for the first few ends, being badly out of practice, but his partner, an accomplished player, had managed to keep the score down to 4-6 on completion of the fifth end. Thereafter Blond got into his stride a little, having been advised by Nigel that he was trying too hard and that he should relax. Taking it a little easier he began to contribute his share to the game.

Blond was surprised that Nigel, Ivor and Peter, none of whom would ever see the age of seventy again, were all 'lads'. It was all 'Good wood, Nige lad' and 'Be up, Ive lad' and 'You're as short as a carrot, Pete lad.' Blond found this quite endearing. In an effort to keep things on this note of informality, and mindful that shortened names seemed to be the status quo in crown green bowls, he told the trio to call him Jim rather than James, with the result that when he was spoken to by the others he was referred to as Jim lad. Blond didn't mind this in the least, although, as it reminded him of young Jim Hawkins being addressed by Long John Silver he found it slightly disconcerting. Just so long as he wasn't threatened with fifty lashes and keel hauling if he didn't shape up!

On completion of the tenth end and with the score at 8-8, or in crown green parlance 8 across, Blond did a little probing. "Is it possible," he casually asked of the ancient trio, "to cheat at this game?"

"Cheat?" said Ivor, as though Blond had asked him if it was possible that brown bears shit in the woods.

"I'll say," piped up Peter, as adamant as Ivor had been incredulous, and proceeded to list some of the methods of cheating. "Walking down the line, going finger with the jack and thumb with your bowl, shifting the mat with your foot when you bowl your second bowl, magic pegs, how many ways of cheating do you want to know about?"

Blond wanted to know about them all, and during the course of the next few ends he did.

Walking up the line, he was informed, was the act of stepping off the mat – the seven inch diameter rubber disc which the bowler stands on to deliver his bowl - after the bowl had been delivered, then following the bowl, thus obscuring from one's opponent its path towards the jack. The opponent could object but by then the damage had already been done. Blond found this useful to know but didn't consider it to be a threat in his upcoming game with Goldnojaws; should he adopt this method of cheating the dwarf was so short that Blond would be able to see over his head with ease, so let him walk up the line to his heart's content. However a genuine threat might come from magic pegs.

Pegs are what players of crown green bowls call the tape measure, and magic pegs are tape measures used in such a way as to cheat one of the bowlers out of a point that is rightfully his. In common with many of the most successful ways of cheating, the method is simplicity itself. The correct way of measuring which bowl is nearer to the jack, on the occasions that it cannot be established with any degree of certainty by the naked eye, is to first take one end of the tape measure to the jack, take the other end to the first bowl to be measured, then lock it in position. The second bowl can then be measured for its proximity to the jack, using the same method. If, when taking the measure to the second bowl it fails to reach it, then the first bowl measured must be the nearer. If it reaches the second bowl and the measure is slack, then the second bowl is the nearer. However, when 'magic' pegs are employed, when the first bowl is measured the measurer only pretends to let out the measure until it reaches the first bowl, but in reality stops short of it, so that when the second bowl is measured it appears to be farther away from the jack than it actually is. The first bowl is thus declared the winner and its owner receives the point that should rightfully go to his opponent. Magic pegs, and the several other ways of cheating divulged by Blond's new friends, would have to be guarded against in the game against Goldnojaws.

Towards the end of the game Nigel suddenly remembered something and said to the others: "Oh by the way lads, I forgot to mention it, the away game against Torkington Park next week is off."

"Off? How come?" said Ivor, surprised.

Peter suspected shenanigans. "I bet the buggers have got people on holiday and they don't want to field a weakened team. I know that Torkington lot."

"No, it's not that. They've had to drop out of the league. The council have sold their green."

Ivor couldn't believe his ears. This was sacrilege. "Sold their green?"

"Straight up. As we were due to play them I went up there for a practice because I haven't played there for a year or two and I wanted to get a feel for the green, that's how I found out. There was a bloke there, told me to sod off, told me I was trespassing. I said who the hell do you think you're telling to sod off? He said 'I'm the man who's just bought this green.'"

Blond had been paying close attention. "Did you get his name?" he said, although he suspected he knew the answer to his question even as he asked it.

"Goldnojaws. He said he was called Goldnojaws. A dwarf he was. No bigger than this." Nigel held his arm out level with his waist. "A right arrogant little prick he was too. He said he'd bought the green for his own personal use. Having a big wooden fence put round it, he said."

Blond considered this latest development. So now Goldnojaws had bought a bowling green to add to his collection of Stockport properties. What on earth did he want with a bowling green? Ostensibly to have a green all to himself according to Nigel but Blond had a gut feeling there was more to it than that.

The game ended shortly afterwards in a narrow 21-19 victory to Peter and Ivor. Nigel and Peter then announced their intention to call it a day; Peter had work to do in his allotment, a load of manure to be dug in, and Nigel had promised to take Jane shopping. So Ivor and Blond embarked on a game of singles. Blond lost 21-14, but not before he had picked up quite a lot of bowling know-how from Ivor, including how to strike – to despatch one's bowl at maximum velocity in an effort to clear the other bowls in the head, a ploy used when there was little or no chance of bettering the bowls already bowled; and how to play a running bowl, employed to shunt an opponent's bowl out of the way, leaving your own bowl nearer the jack. And, most useful of all, he learned how to read a bowling green.

The only features that flat bowling greens and crown bowling greens have in common is that they are roughly the same size and colour. There all similarities end, for whereas a flat green is as flat as its creator can make it a crown green is almost precisely the opposite. The crown, or highest point, is usually, but not necessarily, in the centre of the green, and higher than the rest of the green by up to two feet, occasionally even more. The rest of the green is composed of slopes downwards from the crown to the edges of the green. However within the slopes there are many and diverse undulations, little hills and valleys, humps and hollows, which can cause a bowl to deviate where a flat green would allow it to run straight and true. It has been said, and with more than a grain of truth, that the very best way to build a crown green would be to assemble a gang of Irish navvies and ask them to build a flat green. In short, where a flat green is open, honest and true, a crown green can be as tricky as a barrowful of monkeys. And learning how to read such a green is half the battle to competing with any distinction at the sport.

By the end of the game Blond hoped he had learned enough from Ivor to enable him to do this. And also how to play the game, or at least play it well enough to give Dr Goldnojaws a run for his money. He would very soon find out.

CHAPTER NINE

21 UP

Half past three the following afternoon found James Blond driving the Lada southwards down the A6 towards Torkington Park, just a short distance away from his hotel in the direction of Buxton and the Derbyshire Dales beyond.

Blond's car was another bone of contention, and a bone he fully intended to pick with Maddox on his return to Paramount Properties the very moment he had completed his assignment, and not a moment too soon.

After Blond and Postlethwaite had finished their business in the former's office they had made their way to the underground garage. Blond had fully expected that Postlethwaite wanted to brief him on some new crime-fighting device he'd had fitted to the Lagonda he usually drove on his assignments – the secret agent was aware that an exhaust pipe incorporating a three-inch shell with a nuclear warhead had been on the drawing board for some time – however when they entered the garage Postlethwaite led him straight past his motor car of choice.

"Won't I be taking the Lagonda?" inquired Blond, surprised.

Postlethwaite shook his head. He stopped and pointed to a rusty Lada, fifteen years old if it was a day. "No, you'll be driving that."

"What on earth is that?" said Blond, wrinkling his nose in distaste.

"A Lada."

Blond reeled. "You are joking of course?"

"Afraid not, James. Apparently the department has to be seen to be doing its bit in the Government's current round of cost-cutting and they've specified that the area in which we are to make savings is transport. In effect it means we have to use less expensive cars."

Blond still couldn't quite believe it. "But a Lada for God's sake?"

"Well we needn't have gone that far, I admit. The Minister suggested Mondeos, but Maddox's idea is that if we use really awful cars they'll keep breaking down during your missions."

Blond could scarcely credit it. "I am to be sent out on a mission during which you expect my car to break down?"

"Maddox believes it will make the Government look ridiculous."

"And what about me looking ridiculous? Driving about in a bloody Lada?" said Blond, with feeling.

"It won't be for long I'm sure. The Government will soon see the error of their ways and we'll have you all back in your Astons and Jags in no time. The ploy is already working in fact; SA-Twelve broke down in his twenty-year-old Trebant last week while he was chasing a Barclay's merchant banker and there was hell to pay."

"Riding about in clapped out foreign boneshakers doesn't sit very well with Maddox wanting to raise the profile of the British Secret Service either, I would have thought," said Blond, adding another argument against the Government directive.

"I agree entirely James." Postlethwaite shrugged. "But I'm afraid we'll just have to lump it for the time being."

Blond eyed the Lada. "I assume there are extras with it?"

"Well there's a heater I believe. Not sure if it's working though."

"How about a passenger ejector seat and a pop-up bullet-proof shield for the rear window?"

"I'm afraid not, said Postlethwaite. "Although there is a nodding dog in the back window," he added, with much more enthusiasm than this piece of information warranted.

"Probably giving the nod to my chances of making a bloody fool of myself."

Postlethwaite patted Blond on the shoulder. "I'm sure you'll cope, SA-Seven."

Blond had been forced to accept the situation. Consequently as he headed for Torkington Park he was driving with deep concentration, having found to his cost that driving a Lada without deep concentration was not something to be recommended. The only occasion he'd done it he'd had to turn round and drive back a hundred yards to recover the silencer that had parted company with the rest of the car without warning, and he didn't want that sort of thing happening this morning. Even so, part of his mind was mulling over what had happened recently, or rather had not happened, with Pisa Vass and Divine Bottom.

He could certainly do without it happening again! For one thing there was his reputation to think of; as he had remarked to the lovely Pisa Vass, things like that just do not happen to secret agents, and especially not to James Blond.

Apart from that, and what with one thing and another, he hadn't had sex for over a month, and SA-Seven was a man who liked his fair share of sex, more than his fair share some would say. It was one of the things, along with constantly putting his life at risk, that fuelled him, that made life worth living, and if things were to carry on as they'd been doing for very much longer he would very soon be running on empty.

Earlier that day the most terrible thought had crossed his mind. What if the next girlfriend he propositioned was also having her period? And the next? And the next and the next, and so on and so on, until every one of the next one hundred girlfriends he asked to go to bed with him were similarly cursed. Because it would need that number to redress the balance if, as was the case, none of the previous six hundred had not been having their period.

However despite the ramifications if the situation were to persist Blond was not over-worried; he was aware as much as anyone that for every problem there is a solution, and that in the fullness of time he always came up with that solution. Sure enough, as he nosed the Lada though the narrow entrance to Torkington Park – possibly because it was subliminal, a penis entering a vagina - the answer suddenly came to him.

It was quite simple really when you thought about it. Pisa Vass and Divine Bottom weren't actually girlfriends - because in Blond's book a girl didn't technically become a girlfriend until he had actually slept with her. Problem solved. There still remained the problem that the next ninety eight potential girlfriends might also be menstruating when he asked them if they'd go to bed with him, but the answer to that was equally straightforward. He would simply ask them, prior to propositioning them, if they were having their period. And if they were he wouldn't proposition them. Both problems solved.

Torkington Park is in the Hazel Grove area of Stockport, one of the few parts of the town with pretensions to class. True, graffiti was still evident and plentiful on shop shutters and council house gable ends, but most of it was spelled correctly.

As Blond entered the car park he noticed that a gang of workmen were providing an extra canvas for the graffiti artists of Stockport in the shape of a large fence. Made up of lengths of wood of telegraph pole proportions stood on end, it already surrounded two sides of the bowling green and the workmen were well on their way to completing a third side. The purpose of the fence, if not already clear, was spelt out by the large notice nailed to one of the walls: 'Private Property – Keep Out!', and a similar sized notice:

'Loose Guard Dogs!' Whether the second of the notices meant that the guard dogs in question would be running free within the compound or that they were tied up but had diarrhoea was not made clear, but either of these possibilities presented a terrifying prospect for any would be trespasser.

Once Blond had rounded one of the wooden walls of what was beginning to look like Fort Torkington Park and got his first look at the bowling green he saw that Dr Goldnojaws, accompanied by BloJob and a dowdy-looking woman, had already arrived.

"Only just in time, Mr Bland," said Goldnojaws, tapping his watch meaningfully, on seeing Blond.

"But on time nevertheless," Blond shot back coolly, at once conveying to the dwarf that he wasn't dealing with a man who could be intimidated by people tapping their watches in a stern manner.

Crown green bowlers do not affect the ubiquitous white trousers, shirt and Panama hat favoured in the flat green game, an advantage that is one of its many pleasures. Whatever you feel comfortable in is fine. The occasional bowler has been known to play in jacket and tie but such a person is regarded as an eccentric. Goldnojaws however, without going the whole hog, had chosen to disregard the casual attitude to dress permitted in the crown green game and had made an attempt at looking extra smart, attiring himself in an off-white sweater and slacks and a matching flat cap. The attempt had failed completely, and only drew attention to himself and his lack of height; indeed a distant observer could have mistaken him for a large field mushroom.

BloJob was dressed in exactly the same clothes she had been wearing on both other occasions Blond had seen her. Observing this Blond made a mental note not to stray downwind of her if at all possible.

The older woman, who Blond guessed to be aged around fifty, was dressed in Stockport drab.

Blond had enquired of the assistant at Premier Bowls as to what was regarded as suitable dress for crown green bowls and had been advised to put on whatever came out of the wardrobe first, unless it were a pair of designer jeans, this garment being regarded by some as over-dressing in crown green circles. Consequently he had chosen a navy blue baseball cap, navy blue sweater and light blue Chinos.

Goldnojaws wasted no time on niceties. "BloJob will keep the scores and mark the score card," he said, then, indicating the woman, "Mrs Snockers will assist BloJob with the measuring. If you have no objections, that is?" The inflexion of his voice didn't invite any opposition to his suggestion.

"Not at all," said Blond, then meaningfully, "Why would I possibly object?"

Goldnojaws looked sharply at Blond. His reply was perfunctory. "No reason."

Blond naturally had reservations as to BloJob's honesty, or lack of it, but was not in a position to do very much about it. He would just have to keep a close eye on the Australian's activities in addition to those of Goldnojaws.

"So if you're ready, Mr Bland?" Goldnojaws produced a coin. "We will toss for who will lead out the jack at the first end."

Goldnojaws then made great play of showing Blond both sides of the pound coin, as though to prove to the secret agent that it wasn't a double-headed one, and to therefore demonstrate that everything about him was fair and above board. Blond wasn't fooled for one moment, seeing the elaborate showing of the coin as nothing more than a device to put him off his guard. In fact it had precisely the opposite effect and placed Blond firmly on red alert.

Blond called heads when Goldnojaws tossed the coin and when the one pound piece hit the ground monarch side up was relieved to see he had called correctly. He would need every advantage he could get.

At the first end Blond sent out the jack finger peg, or forehand as it is known in the flat green game, thumb peg and backhand being the other terms for describing the built-in bias of the bowls. The bowl trundled a distance of about thirty yards before coming to rest. Blond then sent the first of his two bowls. It stopped about a yard short and to the right of the jack. Not bad for a loosener thought Blond. Not good enough though, for Goldnojaws' first bowl came to rest inside Blond's bowl by a foot or so. Blond made the necessary adjustment with his next bowl, despatching it with a little more weight and on a slightly narrower line, and almost got it spot on, his bowl narrowly missing the jack and coming to rest about a foot beyond.

"Good bowl Mr Bland," said Goldnojaws. "I can see I shall have to be at my best to beat you."

Or cheat your best, thought Blond, but said: "I am quite sure you will be, Dr Goldnojaws."

Many unlikely people play bowls, among them people who have only one arm or one leg, or even, with the aid of a wheelchair, no legs at all, so Blond didn't think for one moment that Goldnojaws' lack of inches would place him at a disadvantage. Any lingering doubts he may have had about this judgement were dispelled with the delivery of Goldnojaws' second bowl, which was almost perfect, coming to rest mere centimetres from the jack, almost a 'toucher'.

The dwarf turned to Blond and smiled. "One to me, Mr Bland. Game on."

Game on indeed, Blond said to himself, through tight lips.

Goldnojaws turned to BloJob and raised an arm in the air, indicating that he had scored one chalk, and for the Australian to enter it on the scorecard, then he and Blond made their way across the green to the head of bowls.

Bowls, as with golf, is not an overly-physical game, and can be played to a high standard by almost anyone, age, size, shape or strength being of only marginal importance. Skill though is paramount. As with golf, in which it is clubhead speed rather than brute force which propels the ball forward, it is the quality of the bowler's delivery that allows him or her to send the bowl long distances, and with accuracy. Blond was not surprised then when Goldnojaws, having won the right to send the jack out by virtue of winning the previous end, set a long corner mark, up and over the middle of the green, of some forty yards.

"Fancy yourself as a bit of a corner man then do you, Dr Goldnojaws?" remarked Blond, displaying a little of the knowledge and crown green bowls terminology he had picked up the previous day in his games with Ivor, Nigel and Peter.

"I can play corners or the short game and anything in-between, straight peg or round peg, on fast greens or heavy, Mr Bland," said Goldnojaws. "As you will soon discover to your cost." With that he dispatched his bowl. It was played a little over strength and passed the jack by two yards. Blond played his first bowl, short by a yard. As Goldnojaws delivered his second bowl Blond stepped well back from him, in order to see if Goldnojaws attempted any trickery with the mat, one of the ways of cheating he had been warned about.

Moving the mat is a very simple but devastating ploy. In the act of delivering his bowl the player applies downward pressure on the foot which is standing on the mat, then simply slides it across a few inches to the left or right, leaving it in a different position relative to the jack. Not by very much, but enough to cause the second player's delivery to be ever so slightly off line, and very often the difference between it being a winning or losing bowl. However there was not even a hint of Goldnojaws attempting to move the mat, his right foot remaining resolutely on the rubber disc until his bowl had completed its journey. But that was just one delivery, Blond warned himself; his adversary would have many other opportunities to gain an unfair advantage in this way. He would check from time to time to ensure that Goldnojaws kept to his good behaviour.

Goldnojaws looked to have made the correct adjustment with his second bowl but just as it looked as if it were about to roll all the way up to the jack it veered just enough for it to run into the back of Blond's bowl. Goldnojaws cursed his luck. It was the first sign of any petulance from the dwarf. Blond suspected it wouldn't be the last.

Blond sent another quite decent bowl, which bettered both Goldnojaws' bowls, making the score 2-1 in his favour. He turned to BloJob and raised both arms, signalling he had scored two points. Blond noticed that as BloJob entered the score on the card Mrs Snockers looked on, as if to assure herself that BloJob was recording the score correctly. Blond perked up, thinking that he might well have an ally in Mrs Snockers. Excellent.

On the walk to their bowls on completion of the third end, in which Goldnojaws had counted a double, Blond did a little fishing. "So what's so special about Stockport then, Dr Goldnojaws? I mean it's far from the most inviting town in the country from what I've seen of it."

Goldnojaws answered as though what he was saying was common knowledge. "It is without any doubt one of the most uninviting towns in the country, Mr Bland."

"So why buy a shoe manufacturing business here?" Blond paused for just a second before adding casually, "And the local casino too, I believe?"

Goldnojaws looked sharply at Blond. "Have you been spying on me, Mr Bland?"

"Spying?" Blond smiled. "Not at all Dr Goldnojaws. Why would I want to do that? No, I was at the Casino Royale the other night and someone happened to mention it." He paused before going on. "Some people might say you were trying to dominate Stockport." This brought no response from Goldnojaws whatsoever, much to Blond's disappointment. He decided to go for broke and said: "Do you want to dominate Stockport, Dr Goldnojaws?"

Goldnojaws regarded Blond through narrowed eyes for a moment before answering. When he did the beginnings of a smile played on his lips. "That is for me to know, and for you to find out, Mr Bland."

Blond left it at that. Intrigue was obviously Goldnojaws' game. That he should think that Stockport was the most uninviting town in the country yet still want to pitch his tent there was certainly intriguing. And his last remark, 'That is for me to know and for you to find out', although it could have been a way of saying 'Mind your own business' to Blond's way of thinking smacked as more of a challenge.

The score was 8-7 in favour of Goldnojaws when the heron arrived. Flying in from whence it came the large grey and white bird chose a large sycamore by the side of the green on which to alight and spend the next few hours sitting there motionless, as herons are wont to do once their bellies are full and they have put away their harpoon of a beak for the day.

Except that this particular heron didn't sit there motionless. It kept flitting about fitfully from branch to branch every couple of minutes or so, as if unable to decide which of the lofty perches was the more comfortable. On one occasion it happened to be in Goldnojaws' eye line, causing him to stop in mid-delivery of his bowl, almost making him drop it. After cursing the heron under his breath, then waiting until the bird had settled, he retrieved his bowl and carried on with the game. Exactly the same thing happened again two ends later, except that this time Goldnojaws failed to hold on to his bowl and dropped it on his toes. Blond thought the dwarf would lose whatever of his cool remained on this second, more serious, certainly more painful, invasion of his concentration and dignity, but instead he calmly turned to BloJob, barked the single word "BloJob!" and pointed at the heron.

BloJob immediately, and lightning fast, ripped open the front of her shirt, sending buttons pinging in all directions. Then in one continuous motion she tore off her bra, swung it round her head a couple of times and sent it riffling through the air towards the unsuspecting heron with the speed of a Scud Missile. A split second later the heron's head parted company from its body as the bra wrapped itself bolas-like around its neck, cutting through feather, sinew and bone like a knife through butter.

Blond's jaw dropped in amazement. He had been witness to some staggering events during his time in the Secret Service but this piece of pure theatre crowned the lot. The entire sequence from BloJob reaching inside her shirt until the heron's head and body began to make their separate journeys to the ground could not have taken more than five seconds.

Goldnojaws turned his attention back to the bowling match with Blond as though nothing had happened. BloJob, a big smile on her face, but now with a chest as flat as twin pizzas, went to retrieve her cannonball-filled bra. No wonder the crowd of drinkers at the karaoke had gone deathly quiet when BloJob had threatened to remove her bra the other night, thought Blond.

Mrs Snockers now spoke for the first time, concern etched large on her face. "That's cruel! That was cruel, Dr Goldnojaws," she protested. Goldnojaws paid her not the slightest attention and proceeded to deliver his bowl. Mrs Snockers was not to be denied however and made her point. "Do you hear me? Herrings are a protected species."

Goldnojaws turned to her and smiled: "But not protected enough, apparently."

Mrs Snockers sniffed into her handkerchief. "Poor thing. Poor harmless little herring."

"You would be well advised to concern yourself less with the fate of a stupid bird and more with doing the job for which you are paid," snapped Goldnojaws, with an authority that brooked no further protest from Mrs Snockers.

After the incident with the heron the game continued in silence towards its conclusion. It was nip and tuck all the way, neither player ever holding more than a two shot advantage. However it was always Goldnojaws who held the upper hand, with Blond having to claw his way back. Oddly, Blond suspected that sometimes Goldnojaws was getting in front of him then deliberately allowing him to catch up, as if toying with him before finally delivering the coup de grace.

With the score at 18-18, a score at which the game could go either way, Blond had still seen no evidence of any cheating from Goldnojaws. He hadn't walked up the line in an effort to obscure Blond's view, he hadn't tried to move the mat with his foot, he hadn't sent the jack out finger and his bowl out thumb, and the measurers certainly hadn't resorted to using magic pegs. Of that Blond was certain. On the six occasions the measures had been called for he had given the measuring by BloJob and Mrs Snockers his undivided attention and there had not been even the slightest hint of anything untoward. On the last occasion, noticing not for the first time Blond's keen interest in the proceedings, Goldnojaws had asked him why he was paying such close attention. Was he perhaps expecting the measurers to cheat on his, Goldnojaws' behalf? Blond made the excuse that it was only that he was interested in the proceedings, being new to the game, and Goldnojaws seemed to accept his explanation. Because of the incident however Blond now felt pretty sure that he had misjudged Goldnojaws and that the dwarf, unlike Goldfinger, was not a cheat.

By the time the score was tied at 20-20 some five minutes later Blond was even more convinced that Goldnojaws was a better player than he sometimes appeared to be, and was merely stringing him along. During this time Blond had taken the score to 20-18 in his favour with two singles. However they were by no means good singles, Blond's nearest bowl being more than a yard away from the jack on both occasions. Goldnojaws should have beaten it with comfort, but had failed miserably. Then, at the next end, with Blond requiring only one more shot for victory, Goldnojaws produced two near perfect bowls, both ending up almost touching the jack, beating Blond's bowls quite easily. Twenty across and all to play for, Goldnojaws to lead.

Goldnojaws led the jack on his favourite corner mark, a good forty yards. His first bowl ended inches past the jack and just to the right of it. Blond played up. His bowl was equally good, finishing inches short and to the left of the jack. It was by no means clear from a distance of forty yards whose bowl was nearer the jack, and thus lying game. Even with a bowl each still to deliver it was now critical for Goldnojaws to know whose bowl was the nearest; if it was his own bowl then a tactical bowl would be the order of the day, possibly a bowl coming to rest in front of the jack, thus blocking Blond's path to it and leaving his first bowl the winner.

Goldnojaws now walked all the way across the green to inspect the head of bowls. He assessed the situation, taking his time about it, made up his mind what to do, then walked back.

Goldnojaws didn't even look at Blond, let alone give him any intimation as to whose bowl was lying game. In the event he didn't have to, for when the dwarf prepared to strike Blond knew. It was Blond's bowl that was the nearer to the jack. For if Goldnojaws was striking it was either to play Blond's bowl out of the head or to destroy the end – because if it was Goldnojaws' bowl that was the nearer what would be the point of striking?

Goldnojaws wound himself up and sent his bowl hurtling across the green. Blond held his breath. If Goldnojaws' bowl knocked Blond's out of the way it would leave the dwarf's first bowl nearest to the jack. Blond would still have the final bowl, true, but it would be a real pressure bowl, he would have to leave his bowl less than a foot away from the jack from a distance of forty yards.

Blond watched the path of Goldnojaws' bowl with bated breath. Halfway across the green it was a good yard off target. Three-quarters of the way it was still off target, but now by only two feet, the crown of the green having forced it nearer.

But not near enough, and Blond breathed a huge sigh of relief as it sped past the other bowls and clattered into the gutter. Blond had won!

Rather than blow up in a fit of rage, as Blond fully expected he would, Goldnojaws was calmness itself.

He simply turned to Blond, held out his hand and said: "Well played, Mr Bland."

There was nothing left to do but shake Goldnojaws hand, which Blond did, warmly. Clearly he had misjudged the little fellow. "It was a pleasure to play you, Dr Goldnojaws," he said.

With no need now to deliver his last bowl Blond picked up the mat and he and Goldnojaws made their way over to the head of bowls, Blond passing the time of day by remarking how warm it was for the time of the year and Goldnojaws affably concurring. When they were a few yards away from their destination Goldnojaws suddenly stopped, shouted: "BloJob!" and raised an arm in the air, signalling he had scored one point.

Blond gaped. What on earth was going on? "What the....?"

Goldnojaws, with the look of a cat that had got the cream, turned to him and said: "I win."

"What? What do you mean? How can you possibly be the winner?"

"Because my bowl is nearer to the jack than yours, Mr Bland, why do you think?"

Blond was totally confused. "But....but you struck."

"Indeed. But not to hit your bowl or the jack. To miss them, on purpose. Which I did."

Blond looked at the head of bowls. Goldnojaws bowl was clearly nearer to the jack than his, by at least three inches.

Blond now realised he had been tricked, and in spades. And there was not a thing he could do about it, for he had already shaken hands on the game with Goldnojaws; and the dwarf hadn't said "You win" or anything like that, just "Well played, Mr Bland."

So Goldnojaws was a cheat after all! And a more cunning, devious cheat than Goldfinger had ever been, to boot. And if Goldnojaws was a greater cheat than Goldfinger you could bet your bottom dollar he would also turn out to be a greater villain than Goldfinger. Blond would really have to be on the top of his form if he were to bring his latest adversary to book.

Goldnojaws broke into Blond's thoughts. "A thousand pounds I believe we agreed, Mr Bland?"

Blond responded immediately. "Of course." He thought quickly. He had his cheque book with him – his cover extended to his having a checking account in the name of James Bland, the department thought of everything – but he really needed to get another look at Goldnojaws' office. He now took the opportunity to achieve this without creating suspicion. "However," he continued, "I'm afraid I haven't got my cheque book with me. I'll drop by your office tomorrow, if that's all right with you?"

"Whatever." Goldnojaws started to make his way from the green. He called to his factotum: "BloJob."

BloJob fell in beside Goldnojaws as he stepped off the green and together they headed for the car park.

Blond watched them go. He was about to follow them when he realised that Mrs Snockers was still there. He called over to her. "Not leaving with them, Mrs Snockers?"

"No." She pointed at her watch. "It's nearly five-o-clock, my finishing time; there's no point in me going back all the way back to Offerton with them, I only live at Great Moor, just down the road." She joined Blond as he left the green, and said, in a scolding tone: "I must apologise for what that little bugger got BloJob to do to that herring."

Blond put her right. "It's heron, actually, Mrs Snockers. Herrings are what herons eat, if they're lucky."

She smiled. "Yes, I know it's heron really. But I called them herrings when I was a little girl and I never got out of the habit." They walked a little farther. "Talking of herrings has made me hungry. I shan't have anything though or I shall spoil my tea." She explained. "I like to wait for my daughter, Gloria, she doesn't get in from work until seven so we don't eat until about half past." She smacked her lips in anticipation. "Toad-in-the-hole tonight. My favourite."

"Mine too," said Blond, and it was the truth, although it must have been a year since he'd last had it, at his club, Brown's, renowned for its old-fashioned British cuisine.

Mrs Snockers looked at him as if to determine if he was just being polite or if toad-in-the-hole really was his favourite dish. "Is it really?" she asked. Blond nodded. "Then you must join us," she said generously.

"Oh I wouldn't dream of imposing on you."

"No I insist," said Mrs Snockers, no nonsense. "You'll love it. I do a lovely toad- in-the-hole; plenty of toad in it, not nearly all hole like supermarket toad-in-the-hole." A thought struck her. "And you'll be able to meet my lovely daughter Gloria too. I'm sure you'll like her."

How could a man resist? Toad-in-the-hole with plenty of toad in it and the lovely Gloria Snockers seated across the table from him? No contest. "I thank you very much and accept your generous invitation, Mrs Snockers," smiled Blond. By now they had reached the car park. He indicated the Lada. "Can I go some way to repaying your kindness by offering you a lift?"

Mrs Snockers clapped her hands in delight on seeing Blond's car. "Oh, a Lada," she squealed. "I had sex for the very first time on the back seat of a Lada."

Too much information, thought Blond, only just managing not to pull a face. Fifty-year-old women having sex on the back seat of a Lada conjured up the kind of vision he could well do without.

"Shall I get in the back?" asked Mrs Snockers eagerly, her hand already on the door handle. For one horrible moment Blond thought Mrs Snockers wanted him to join her for sex on the back seat, but she continued: "It'll be just like I'm being chauffeured."

Blond smiled. "But of course, Mrs Snockers." He opened the door for her and she climbed in. Blond got in the driver's seat and turned to her. "Where to, madam?"

CHAPTER TEN

FOR YOUR EYES ONLY

The A4 Manila envelope from Maddox was delivered to Blond by hand. Although halfway through shaving prior to his dinner date with the Snockers he dealt with it immediately, communications from Maddox delivered in such a manner being always of the utmost importance, code red. This one was no different; written on the envelope in large red lettering were the words 'For Your Eyes Only'.

Blond ripped open the envelope. Inside was a DVD of the Bond movie of than name. He grimaced. Why on earth would he want such a thing? Maddox must have known he would have already seen it. The old fool must have sent it to him as a reminder for him to try to be more like James Bond. Disdainfully he threw the DVD into the waste bin.

He returned to the bathroom and finished shaving. He was about to apply his personal after-shave, made especially for him by Marcel of Knightsbridge, when Maddox's voice suddenly emanated from the waste bin: "Don't be such a twat Blond and open the bloody DVD case!"

Blond hurried to the waste bin and retrieved the DVD. He opened the case. The first thing he saw was the tiny transmitter through which Maddox had just addressed him, obviously timed to be activated five minutes after the envelope had been opened if no action had been taken by then. Blond inspected the disc. Stuck to the back of it was a small brown envelope. Inside the envelope were three pages of close typescript. He began to read.

To: SA-7

From: M

Copies to: N,O,P,Q,R,S,T,U,V,W,X,Y and Z.

Thanks to: My agent Tom Gilman at Secret Agents Management, without whose invaluable help this would not have been possible; my manager Abe Silverstein, thanks Abe; my lovely wife Beth for loving me and allowing me to love her and for her unstinting encouragement when things were at their lowest ebb in the darkest hours; my Mum and Dad for having me; my Nana for looking after me while Mum went out to work; my friends and colleagues in MI6 for placing their blind faith and absolute trust in me; The Home Secretary for giving me the job in the first place; my postman for delivering the letter informing me I'd got the job; the postman's wife for looking after him, therefore enabling him to deliver the letter informing me that I'd got the job; my butcher, my baker, my candlestick maker, Old Uncle Tom Cobbleigh and all …. altogether please… and Old Uncle Tom Cobbleigh and all!

Subject:- Dr Uric Goldnojaws.

Real name Carl Denis St John Davis III. Born St Thomas's Hospital, Stockport, March 9, 1965. Father, Carl Denis St John Davis II, son of Carl Denis Terence St John Davis and Amy Dodds, nee Horrocks. Mother Alice Davis, nee Trembler.

Carl Denis St John Davis III's was a difficult birth as his mother was in labour for almost two days before the doctors realised she still had her tights on. The Davises were a poor family, and for the first five years of his life Carl was confined to the house as his parents couldn't afford to buy clothes for him. Then on his fifth birthday they bought him a hat so he could lean out of the window. This encouraged him to venture outside, where he immediately began to terrorise the neighbourhood, eventually coming to be known as Carl the Hat. Money gained from his crimes soon enabled him to buy a full set of clothes and thereafter he was known as Carl the Hat Scarf Overcoat Jacket Trousers Shirt Vest Underpants Socks and Shoes. His activities first brought him to the notice of the police in 1971 when he stole a small pink toilet trainer from the Stockport branch of Mothercare and was charged with potty theft. The case was tried at Stockport Potty Sessions where he was fined and cautioned as to his future behaviour. The swearing in took an unusually long time because he swore on the card and read the bible. He said to the judge 'I do not recognise this court'. The judge said 'Why not?' He said 'You've had it decorated.' He was sentenced to two years in prison. He was a model prisoner and occasionally walked down the catwalk modelling new jail uniforms and suits for those prisoners about to be paroled. Eighteen months later he himself was paroled.

It is a common belief that the thing a man most desires on being released from prison is a home cooked meal. This is a misconception. The first thing a man wants on being released from prison is sex. The second thing he wants is also sex. And the third. The fourth thing he wants is a home cooked meal, quickly followed by sex, but often at the same time, narrowly beating into fifth place even more sex.

When Carl was finally set free he was no different than any other man in this respect. What he needed, and fast, was a woman. Any woman. A prostitute would be fine. A prostitute would be preferred in fact, because you don't have to bullshit them or buy them presents or treat them to dinner or be nice to them first. However he had a problem inasmuch as all he had to his name on being released from Strangeways were a pair of plimsolls and a ten pence piece. On the streets of Manchester he approached a prostitute. "How much do you charge?" he asked. "Five pounds," she replied. "I've only got ten pence and a pair of plimsolls," said Carl. "Ten pence and a pair of plimsolls?" scoffed the prostitute. "I'm not doing it for that; what do you take me for?" Carl pleaded with her, explaining that he was newly released from prison and desperate for the comfort of a woman. The prostitute softened to his story. "Well all right then," she said. "But there won't be any passion. You can't expect any passion for ten pence and a pair of plimsolls." However Carl wasn't bothered that the liaison would be passionless on her part, he had enough passion for the both of them. She took him to his flat, and without ceremony, but with a condom, they got on the bed and started to make love. After a very short while the prostitute's arms came up and around Carl and her legs rose off the bed and wrapped tightly round him. Carl smirked and said to the prostitute "I thought you said there wouldn't be any passion?" She said "I'm trying on the plimsolls."

Thereafter nothing is known of Carl Davis III until he turned up in Russia in 1990 where he eventually became an agent for SMESH and SMASH. SMESH is a conjunction of the two Russian words Smesta and Shentiv, which roughly means death to enemies of the USSR. SMASH means death by eating crappy synthetic mashed potatoes. The only other light that can be thrown ......

There the typescript suddenly stopped, to be replaced by Maddox's neat handwriting.

Sorry about the above, James. The thing is the Blind Date scriptwriter was at something of loose end so we put him to work compiling this dossier. As you can see he made a real dog's breakfast of it, exchanging diligent investigation and fact gathering for cheap cracks he'd either stolen or made up (I suspect the former as I've heard the one about the ten pence and the pair of plimsolls before. I quite liked the one about his mother still having her tights on though). All the same I have included it as it might cheer you up a bit as you must be pretty miserable up there.

The thing is, the only truth in what you have read thus far is that our friend Dr Goldnojaws was born in Stockport; which may well have something to do with why he now wants to dominate it. Maybe in the past he was wronged in some way by the town and now wants to exact his revenge?

The only other thing we know for certain is that he is seriously rich. His money comes from Russian oil, and was acquired in much the same dubious way in which Chelsea football boss Roman Abramovich and similar Russian oligarchs came by their billions. Goldnojaws' riches are not of the order of Abramovich's but he is reckoned by our chaps in the Foreign Office to be worth at the very least one billion pounds. Up to now he has managed to keep low key about his wealth.

And that's just about it, all we've been able to find out about him, try as we might. So it's up to you now James. I'm sure you'll come up trumps. Chin up.

Having committed the contents of the dossier to memory Blond, following MI6 standard procedure, ripped it into tiny shreds, dropped it in the lavatory pan, peed on it, then flushed it down the toilet. The peeing on it wasn't part of the procedure but because he needed a pee, at least twenty minutes having passed since he'd had the last one. He really must do something about his blasted prostate! Was there a solution that didn't involve the knife? Drugs or diet perhaps? He would find out just as soon as he got back to London. He certainly couldn't go on like this for much longer.

He checked the time. He had an hour to kill. He used it to go through the events thus far.

The facts as he saw them were that a Dr Goldnojaws, obviously a false name, a man who kept himself to himself, had recently returned to his home town of Stockport. Once there, and in a very short time, he had bought a shoe factory, a casino, the local football club, a bowling green and the air raid shelters complex. These were acquisitions Blond knew about. There could be more. But what had the man done wrong? Nothing so far as Blond could see. He was buying property, something that business entrepreneurs do all the time. And what a man does with his money is his own business, even though, as Maddox had reported, the money was ill-gotten.

And if that was all that was meant by Goldnojaws' dominating Stockport there was nothing to be done about it, and even less to worry about. Unless he wanted to dominate Stockport for some other reason? Unless he had a hidden, sinister agenda. Which he must have, otherwise why would he call himself Dr Goldnojaws, a name made up from the names of villainous fictional characters? Blond thought about it for a few minutes more but nothing came up. It would eventually, he was sure.

He checked his appearance in the mirror. His hair wasn't quite perfect so he re-combed it and dressed it with his hairspray, especially made for him by Coiffzone of Bristol. Finally he charged his wallet with a three pack of condoms, especially made for him by the London Rubber Company, and set out for his dinner date with Mrs and Gloria Snockers.

CHAPTER ELEVEN

GLORIA SNOCKERS

Whenever Blond was in London he drank his own burgundy, especially made for him by Domaine Camille-Giroud of Beaune, but this was Stockport so Sainsbury's had had to suffice. Nevertheless he found a very acceptable domaine-bottled Nuits St Georges from the superb 1988 vintage and it was a bottle of this wine that Blond presented to Mrs Snockers on arriving at her brick built, ivy–clad, semi-detached property on Greenheys Lane shortly before seven thirty.

"Oh you shouldn't have bothered Mr Bland," scolded Mrs Snockers, taking the bottle off Blond, before adding: "Although I must confess I do like a nice glass of red of an evening. Australian is it?"

Blond inwardly shuddered at the suggestion that anyone might think he was such a cheapskate as to palm a host off with what the Australians laughingly call wine. (Blond had once drunk a glass of Australian red wine by mistake and it had given him an upset stomach for a week; although it is true to say that his doctor had suggested that the more likely cause of Blond's discomfort might be rooted in the secret agent's deep prejudice against new world wines rather than the contents of the bottle.) He gave no sign of this to the woman who had been kind enough to offer him dinner however, his good breeding preventing this. "I'm afraid the wine shop didn't have any Australian wine, Mrs Snockers," he smiled. "Must have had a run on it, can't say I'm surprised, so I had to make do."

"Shame. But never mind, I'm sure this will be very nice," said Mrs Snockers, looking dubiously at the label, noting the year of the wine and possibly looking for a 'best before' date. "Even if it is a bit old." She started to fuss again. "Now sit yourself down and make yourself at home. Oh and by the way, just in case you was wondering. There isn't a Snockers. He died a few years back."

Blond offered his commiserations. "I'm sorry."

"You've no need to be, he was a pig, a wastrel if ever there was one. Spent half his life in the betting shop and the other half hiding from people he'd borrowed money off of so he could go to the betting shop in the first place. I'm better off without him, believe you me. No, the only good thing he did in his entire life was give me my Gloria. And that was the bestest thing." She made to head for the kitchen when a thought struck her. "Oh and just in case you was thinking; I'm not looking for a husband. I invited you for your tea because you seem like a nice man and you like toad-in-the-hole; I mean I'm not setting my cap at you or anything like that." She paused for a moment then smiled coyly. "Mind you, I can't speak for my Gloria." With that Mrs Snockers disappeared into the kitchen with the bottle of burgundy, calling out on her way: "Gloria, that nice Mr Bland gentleman is here."

Blond sat down in one of the easy chairs and automatically set about taking an inventory of the room, paying particular attention to the location of the doors and windows. Though obviously not in a threatening environment he could not help himself but go through this routine, years in the Secret Service seeing to that; it was a procedure he always went through on entering a strange room in case he should have to make a quick exit, a policy that had paid dividends on more than one occasion.

Blond had just completed his examination of the room and was admiring the flight of brown and yellow pot ducks winging their way up Mrs Snockers' floral wallpapered chimney breast when he heard the sound of footsteps coming downstairs. Seconds later Gloria Snockers entered the room. Immediately making a quick exit was the very last thing in the world Blond wished to do.

As apt as Divine Bottom's name had been it was no more appropriate than that of Gloria Snockers. She was quite simply the possessor of quite the most magnificent pair of breasts Blond had ever had the privilege to set eyes on.

And it was a privilege indeed. All men are either leg men or tit men. Blond himself had always been a leg man, considering a nice pair of breasts to be a bonus rather than the main attraction in his women, but there was no way on earth that Gloria Snockers' breasts could be looked upon as a mere bonus. Unfettered by a bra, thrusting against the thin cotton of her snow white top, each breast was thrillingly separate, although, as with fine antiques, they were much more desirable as a pair. The breasts were large, but not too large. Blond intuitively knew that underneath the skimpy top her nipples would be like two bright red cherries; they were certainly the size of cherries. The shape of the breasts was perfection itself. If Michelangelo had forsaken all his works of art and devoted his entire life to sculpting a perfectly shaped pair of breasts he could not have chiselled out anything finer; the perfect concave curve down to the nipple being matched in sweeping elegance by the convex curve that was the underside of her breast, the two breasts tilted so that the nipples pointed slightly upwards. Blond could see that a man could easily have hung his hat on one of the breasts and his umbrella on the other. But what a criminal waste of such a beautiful, wonderful pair of breasts that would have been. Breasts such as these were not for hanging a gentleman's hat and umbrella on, they were for gazing upon, fondling, stroking, gently squeezing, licking and sucking.

"Hello, you must be Mr Bland," smiled the girl. "I'm Gloria."

Blond tore his eyes away from Gloria's breasts for long enough to take in her pretty face and short honey blonde hair. Her hair gave her an elfin, almost gamin look, in contrast to her body, which was all woman. Together the combination was devastating. She was aged about nineteen, fresh-faced, vibrant, her baby blue eyes shining with health. Even if her breasts had been just a common or garden pair of breasts she would have been very desirable. But with those wonderful orbs, which Blond now found himself looking at once again to ensure he hadn't been dreaming, she was truly out of this world.

Gloria smiled again and looked down at the objects of Blond's fascination. "Nice aren't they."

Blond blushed, embarrassed, and stammered: "I....I wasn't...."

"It's all right," she broke in, "I don't mind, I'm used to it by now." Then, with a look over her shoulder to make sure her mother's return wasn't imminent, she took hold of the bottom of her white top and pulled it up under her chin, revealing her breasts in all their naked glory. "There you go, have a good look."

Blond's jaw dropped. Unclothed Gloria's breasts were even more wonderful than they had promised to be. She held the pose for about five seconds, which to Blond seemed both like an eternity and a nanosecond at one and the same time, before pulling the top down. At the very moment Gloria covered herself up again one of the ex-Blind Date scriptwriter's one-liners for occasions such as this, 'Thanks for the Mammaries', fought its way to the forefront of his mind, but Blond, so utterly enchanted by what he had witnessed, didn't wish to cheapen the moment. He simply said. "Thank you for that, Gloria. I am truly most grateful."

"That's all right," smiled Gloria. "I know men like looking at my breasts, and it doesn't do anyone any harm, does it."

Blond was thinking that it certainly hadn't done him any harm and was about to congratulate Gloria on her refreshing attitude when Mrs Snockers popped her head through the kitchen doorway. "Tea's ready, you two. We eat in the kitchen Mr Bland, I hope you don't mind?"

Blond would have been quite content to eat in the coalplace, dining off the coalplace floor even, if it had meant it would put him in the company of Gloria Snockers and her wonderful breasts. "Not at all, Mrs Snockers, not at all," he smiled. "And please, call me James. You too Gloria."

The toad-in-the-hole was delicious, the Nuits St Georges a perfect if incongruous partner. It was served with creamed mashed potatoes, a robust and flavourful onion gravy and mushy peas.

It was Blond's introduction to mushy peas and he was quite surprised at their taste when he popped a forkful into his mouth, not least because his taste buds had been expecting guacamole. Noticing the shocked expression on his face Mrs Snockers told him to spit out the peas if he didn't like them, she wouldn't be offended, not everyone liked mushies, but Blond assured her that quite to the contrary the northern delicacy was delightful.

In fact the whole plateful, and it was indeed a plate full, along with the jam roly poly that followed, ensured that Blond had not dined better in ages. Then, as if that wasn't enough, Blond's cup truly began to runneth over. For no sooner the meal was over Mrs Snockers announced she would have to leave them to it, she was very sorry, she hoped Blond would forgive her, it was her bingo night and that life-size pot giraffe she'd had her eye on for some time hadn't been won yet.

After Mrs Snockers had left in her quest for the pot giraffe, with a departing mock admonishment of "Now don't do anything I wouldn't do" and a cheery "That doesn't leave us much scope, Mum", from her daughter,

Blond and Gloria engaged in small talk while he helped her clear the table and wash the dishes. He discovered that she worked at a health club, she'd been there since leaving school, she loved it and couldn't ever imagine doing anything else. She liked clubbing, especially the Heaven and Hell Club at Stockport Grand Central – she described the club with its two floors of dance and trans music and its alcopops; Blond could see several reasons why the club was called Hell but not a single reason why it would be called Heaven. She liked going to rock gigs, partying and 'having a laugh'.

As it was abundantly clear that the lovely Gloria was his for the taking without the need to improve his chances by letting it be known that he was James Blond, a glamorous secret service agent - which was guaranteed to overcome any resistance - Blond simply went along with his cover and told her he was sales director of L for Leather.

After they'd finished the dishes and then, seated side by side on the settee, what was left of the Nuits St Georges, Blond took hold of Gloria's hand, looked deep into her eyes, and made his play. "You are a beautiful girl, Gloria."

"Thank you, kind sir," she breathed, pleased at the compliment.

He put his arm round her shoulder. She wriggled closer to him. He whispered in her ear. "I would like to make love to you." She smiled up at him, lovingly. He went on: "But first I must ask you something."

"Yes?"

"Are you menstruating?"

She looked at him as though she couldn't quite believe what he had said and took some time to reply. Finally she said: "No. No I'm not."

Blond smiled. "I had to ask you, Gloria."

Gloria went on. "No, I've never hated men, I love men."

Blond's brow creased in puzzlement. Never hated men? What was she talking about? Then he realised Gloria's mistake. He smiled. "No, I didn't ask you if you were men hating, Gloria my love. I asked you if you were menstruating."

"Yes," said Gloria, "that's what I thought you said. I was just giving you the benefit of the doubt in case I hadn't heard you right." And with that she slapped him round the head so hard he fell off the settee. His ears rang for the next ten minutes.

CHAPTER TWELVE

THE PIED PIPER

The gents' toilet at the Façade factory was off the reception area. As was the case with his initial visit Blond had to call in there for a pee before presenting himself to Dr Goldnojaws. While he was relieving himself he noted that the lavatory was a Twyfords Rampart. On his previous visit he had used another of the three stalls, where the lavatory had been an Armitage Shanks. One of them was obviously a replacement, mused Blond, probably the Twyfords, which was of a more modern design than the Armitage.

Since he'd started having trouble with his prostate gland Blond, having the need of them as frequently as he did, had become something of an authority on the subject of lavatories. He could now identify in excess of forty different designs and systems, along with their manufacturer, although the pleasure of encountering an example of the first water closet to be manufactured in any quantity, the Thomas Crapper, still awaited him. In fact so knowledgeable had Blond become that if were to go on Mastermind he could have taken lavatories as his specialist subject, 'James Blond, three minutes on the lavatory, your time starts….now'.

A couple of minutes later, freshly drained, found the secret agent walking through into the reception area. The secretary was at her desk. He approached her. "I'd like to see Dr Goldnojaws, if I may?"

"I'm afraid he isn't in at the moment. Was the doctor expecting you?"

"I have a cheque for him."

The secretary held out her hand. "If you could let me have it I'll make sure he gets it," she said, all efficiency and horn-rimmed glasses.

The secretary's competence was something Blond could have done without, her incompetence would have been much more preferable. He needed to get into Goldnojaws' office for a good look round, another look at the large wall map of Stockport being one of his priorities. In fact Goldnojaws being out could work to his advantage; if he could spend a little time alone in the office it would serve his purposes even better.

"Why don't I just leave it on his desk?" said Blond smoothly, taking the cheque from the inside pocket of the jacket of his suit, especially made for him by Jenkins of Savile Row, and making for Goldnojaws' office door.

The secretary sprang to her feet as if her life depended on it and rushed to bar his way. "No! I'm afraid that won't be possible. Not even I am allowed in Dr Goldnojaws' office on my own."

With his extensive knowledge of the body's pressure points Blond could have easily, in the bat of an eyelid, rendered the secretary unconscious for the next half hour. However such a course of action would draw attention to him. So he merely contented himself by saying: "In that case I will wait for Dr Goldnojaws' return."

"If you insist," said the secretary, far too snootily for Blond's liking. He looked forward to taking her down a peg or two if and when the chance presented itself.

In the event Goldnojaws' absence turned out to be a blessing.

The previous night he had apologised to Gloria Snockers, she had graciously accepted his apology, they became friends again, he had asked her if she would make love with him, she said she would have but she was having her period, he had returned to the Cheshire Towers to drown his sorrows. To take his mind off that heartbreaking event he surveyed the Façade factory floor again. He really did need to discover what it was that didn't seem quite right about it. He failed in this objective, but he did discover something of possibly even greater importance. The identity of the man in the white overall.

While Blond was weighing up the interior dimensions of the factory floor the man came through the same door from which he had emerged on his previous visit. However this time the man didn't turn back but walked the full length of the factory floor before going through a door at the far end. Limping ever so slightly, Blond now noted.

It was the limp that jogged Blond's memory, the piece of the jigsaw previously missing. It had failed to register with him when he had very briefly seen the man the first time. But once he had spotted it and married it to the dark, swarthy features of its owner, Blond was in no doubt as to his identity. It was his old adversary, Professor Gonzalez.

Gonzalez had been in the employ of a villain in one of Blond's previous adventures, the Dr Zog case. Dr Zog was yet another manifestation of the crazed individual who wants to take over the world. His plan was twofold. First he would make the world's supply of cheese addictive; that is, much more addictive than it already was to the average cheese-lover. This he would achieve by adding highly concentrated heroin to the curds and whey during the cheese manufacturing process. The resultant cheese would be of such narcotic intensity that if anyone were to eat just a few crumbs they would be hooked on it immediately and in a very short space of time become a hopeless addict, either of cheese, heroin or both. Having achieved this objective Dr Zog would then put the second part of his fiendish plan into operation.

A race of cheese-loving super rats had been bred, rats not as big as cats but as big as racehorses, each of them as fast as if they had Frankie Detori up and laying on with the whip. The super rats would now be unleashed on the cheese and heroin addicted public. The public would compete with the rats for the cheese, in the process of which they would become hopeless addicts. The cheese supplies would very soon run out, panic would reign in the streets, carnage would quickly follow. In the quest for food man would fight man, rat would fight rat, man would fight rat and rat would fight man until each and every one of both species had perished from their wounds, from hunger or from drug addiction. It was a quite dazzling plan.

All the above would take place in one country at a time. Dr Zog had calculated that after it had happened to three minor countries the world's leaders would be ready to listen to his terms. His terms were simple; himself at the top of the pile and everyone else a long way beneath him.

Professor Gonzalez, a brilliant bio chemist and genetic engineer, had been one of the team of scientists assembled by Dr Zog to produce the race of super rats in their millions.

Wales was the unfortunate country chosen to be the testing ground for Dr Zog's diabolical plan. He chose it not because the Welsh are amongst the biggest cheese eaters in the world, nor because it is the home of the world famous Caerphilly cheese, nor even because it is also the home of Welsh Rarebit, but simply because he hated Welshmen.

The reason for his hatred of Welshmen and all things Welsh was simple. Some time ago he'd had the misfortune to be trapped in a railway carriage on a journey from London to Cardiff with a dozen Welsh rugby supporters who had earlier that day seen their team defeat England at Twickenham. Each and every one of this motley crew, like all Welshmen, imagined he could sing, and proceeded to prove that he couldn't from the moment the party got on the train until it arrived in Cardiff four hours late, some six hours later.

At the time of the incident Dr Zog's plans for world domination were well underway and after being forced to listen to Bread of Heaven six times and Land of my Father eight times Gonzalez consoled himself in the knowledge that these particular Welshmen would not have bread from Heaven nor fathers to sing about for much longer, as they would very soon be pushing up the daisies.

The plan was duly put into operation and after only two weeks the entire population of Wales had become cheese addicts. The first five thousand giant rats were then released and began to compete for the cheese.

Up until the release of the rats, despite shortages here and there due to the increased demand, the populace was still managing to satisfy its hunger for cheese by buying it from supermarkets, delicatessens and specialty cheese shops; but rats as big as racehorses don't have to conform to such conventions as buying. They dictate their own marketing agenda. This being the case the entire stocks of cheese at all branches of Asda and Morrison's and Sainsbury's and Waitrose soon disappeared faster than it takes to make a supermarket sweep; speciality cheese shops were cleaned out in a matter of minutes; delicatessens were rendered cheeseless in less time than it takes to say "Eight ounces of blue stilton please and not too much crust if you don't mind, you gave me nearly all crust the last time." The only cheese the rats ignored were the slices to be found in Big Mac Cheeseburgers, which could of course only be consumed along with the rest of the contents of the Big Mac, and which the rodents not surprisingly declined to do, thus confirming the popularly held belief that rats are highly intelligent.

Observing the wholesale carnage from the safety of London, the Government acted immediately. The top brains in the country were brought together and a plan of action worked out and put into effect.

The first idea was giant rat traps. Ten thousand six feet long by four feet wide wooden spring-loaded rat traps were baited with cheese and laid on the pavements of Cardiff, Swansea, Newport and Neath. The following day they were withdrawn when it was discovered they had trapped more Welshmen than rats, the cheese bait being as much of an attraction to the former as it was to the latter but the rats being more adept at avoiding the traps.

Selective bombing was then tried, but with only limited success, and at the cost of over a quarter of the Principality's houses.

By this time the United Nations had become involved and at the suggestion of the Director General of that august body a crack team of United States Army marksmen were brought in to shoot the rats. Exhibiting their usual expertise with small arms they too accounted for more Welshmen than rats and were quickly withdrawn.

US President Barack Obama and Secretary of State Hillary Clinton sent their commiserations to the Welsh and expressed their hope that the terrible situation in the Welsh nation's homeland of Scotland would soon return to normal.

In yet another effort to solve the problem every household in Wales was issued with a week's supply of bottled water. Warfarin was then introduced into the entire nation's reservoirs and water pumping stations, the idea being that the rats would drink it and perish. Unfortunately the vast quantities of fluoride already in the water killed the Warfarin before it could kill the rats.

At this point a prominent right wing Member of Parliament proposed bringing back both the giant rat traps and the US Army marksmen, as the United Kingdom could only benefit from there being a few hundred thousand less Welshmen, and while this seemed to the Government to be a wholly sensible suggestion it was not taken up as it might have had the effect of supplying ammunition to Plaid Cymru and there was a General Election coming up in the not too distant future.

Finally, and not before time in Blond's opinion, the Secret Service was brought in. SA-Eight was charged with stopping the supply of heroin-laced cheese, while it was left to SA-Seven, James Blond, to rid the world of the giant rats.

It took Blond just thirty six hours into the assignment to discover where the rats were being bred - a disused underground ammunition dump in Kent, a relic of the Second World War, close to the White Cliffs of Dover.

He quickly evolved a plan; to cut off the problem at its source, thus ensuring that no more giant rats could be bred, then, having done that, to exterminate the five hundred thousand rats that had already been bred and were on hold, to be released on Dr Zog's orders.

Cutting off the problem at its source would be a piece of cake. Ten judiciously-placed pounds of plastic explosive would see to that. But how to rid the world of half a million giant rats? More explosives? Not without blowing up half of Kent along with them. And it wasn't the Welsh valleys, which were expendable, that we were talking about here, this was the Garden of England. Poison the rats? A possibility; but half a million? The poison would take time to work and even then there would be the problem of getting rid of the poisoned rotting bodies, with the accompanying risk to public health. No, the situation called for something daring, something innovative and imaginative.

Eventually Blond came up with the very thing, but when he did, although daring, it was neither innovative nor imaginative in the slightest. Merely the application of a lesson learned from the pages of history.

Once the Semtex had done its job, completely destroying the rat breeding plant and killing all the people who worked in it with the exception of Professor Gonzalez, who had been away at the time, Blond rode into the vast underground cavern on his 1000cc motor bike, especially made for him by Harley Davidson of York. Seated on the pillion of the gleaming machine was not a passenger but a fifty pounds block of ripe cheese, especially made for him by St Ivel of Swindon. Blond rode the Harley round the perimeter of the vast pack of giant rats at a steady five miles-per-hour, exposing the rats on the edges of the pack a good whiff of the cheese, then, gradually increasing speed, he set off for the entrance of the cavern, one hand on the handle bars the other hand holding a pipe on which he commenced to play a merry tune; an unnecessary touch but one that appealed to Blond's sense of humour. As one, the five hundred thousand strong pack of giant rats started to follow him. Once he was out in the open air Blond, as comfortable astride a motor bike as he was astride a woman, settled to a steady forty miles-per-hour.

He looked over his shoulder to ensure all the rats were following him. They were. He estimated the distance between his back wheel and the leading rats. It was about thirty yards, just about right, near enough for the leading rats to see him and smell the cheese on the pillion, but far enough away from their snapping jaws for comfort. He reckoned his present speed would maintain the distance separating them, but would make frequent checks.

After the Harley had eaten up about a mile Blond left the metalled road for the open countryside. Now the surface under his speeding wheels was grass interspersed with small outcrops of the white limestone for which the famous White Cliffs are named.

It was those very cliffs, and the cruel sea below and beyond them, to which Blond now pointed the Harley. He checked behind him again. The rats were still following. He accelerated up to forty five miles-per-hour to determine if they could keep up with him. He wanted them moving as fast as possible when they hit the cliff's edge. After lagging behind momentarily before they adjusted to the new speed the rats maintained the gap. Blond pushed the speed up to fifty. The rats responded, but looked to be right at their limit. Blond smiled, fifty miles per hour would do just fine.

Ahead of him Blond could see the edge of the cliffs, beyond it nothing but the distant horizon. Two hundred yards from the sheer two hundred and fifty feet drop he began to decelerate. Forty miles-per-hour, thirty, twenty. He looked over his shoulder. The leading rats were now only five yards away from his back wheel, their crazed yellow eyes boring into him. But Blond and the Harley were by now only yards from the edge of the cliffs with nothing beyond but space. He wound up the throttle and with a roar the Harley picked up speed and soared off the end of the cliffs and into the ether. The rats, like so many gigantic lemmings, blindly followed him over the edge, wave upon wave of them, like some enormous furry waterfall cascading into the ice-cold English Channel below.

Letting go of the handlebars Blond allowed the Harley to slip away from under him and fall into the sea along with the rats. It had done its work, and well. Harley Davidson and England could be proud of it.

Blond now pulled the ripcord of his parachute. A second later there was a satisfying clunk and a fierce but comforting tug on the harness as the parachute billowed open. The south-westerly wind which prevailed that day blew the parachute away from the cliffs and because of this about ten seconds had elapsed before Blond hit the water. At exactly the same moment, and to his great satisfaction, he saw the last of the giant rats throw themselves off the cliff's edge into the foaming sea below, and certain death. History had been revisited. The Pied Piper had struck again!

The ringing of the secretary's phone brought Blond back to the present. He checked his watch. He had been waiting for half-an-hour and still there was no sign of Goldnojaws.

The more Blond thought about it the more he was convinced that a short time alone in Goldnojaws' office would be of more benefit than any amount of time spent there whilst Goldnojaws was in residence. He came to a decision. First the stumbling block of Goldnojaws' secretary would have to be removed. But how to accomplish this? Blond gave the matter his full concentration. A solution soon presented itself. "I'm just popping out for some cigarettes, I appear to have run out," he said to the secretary.

The secretary looked at him with a deliberate show of indifference and remained silent. She'll be silent for a lot longer than she wants to be in a short while, Blond promised himself, as he made for the door.

Blond had previously noticed a corner shop on the street next to Façade. He hoped it sold chocolates. It did. He bought a large box of Black Magic.

On his return to Façade he went to the Gents' toilet once more. After locking himself into one of the stalls and having another pee he removed the cellophane paper from the box of chocolates and opened it. From force of habit he took out the Turkish Delight and dropped it down the lavatory; he had loathed this particular confection as a boy and had discovered over the years that it was an aversion he shared with everyone else. He then removed his right shoe, especially made for him, along with his left shoe, by Barkers of Peterborough, and twisted the heel through ninety degrees to reveal the secret cavity within. He extracted a miniature syringe. In the syringe was a powerful Mickey Finn, especially made for him by Mickey Finn of Dublin. Carefully he injected a small amount of the knockout drug into each of the top row of chocolates, replaced the dark brown corrugated paper cover, closed the box and returned it to his pocket.

The secretary was gossiping on the phone when Blond got back. He waited patiently until she'd finished, then opening the box of Black Magic he casually approached her desk. He held the box out to her and said temptingly: "Chocolate?"

She looked up at him suspiciously.

Blond urged her, pushing the box towards her. "Please. I would feel guilty eating chocolates without first offering them around."

The secretary put her suspicion to one side, nodded, and reached for the box.

Blond smiled. His plan was going to work. He had been certain it would; if any woman could resist chocolate he had yet to meet her. In next to no time the secretary would be dead to the world and he would be in Goldnojaws' office.

The secretary removed the corrugated paper and looked at the chocolates in the box. Her brow wrinkled. "Where's the Turkish Delight?"

"Pardon?"

"The Turkish Delight is missing."

Blond feigned surprise. "Is it?" What did the silly bitch want with a Turkish Delight?

"It is," she said, replacing the corrugated paper and pushing the box away. "Thanks all the same but I only like Turkish Delight."

Blond saw his best laid plans sinking without trace. It was straw clutching time. "The coffee crème is very toothsome," he suggested.

"No, I only like Turkish Delight."

"The praline pate is to die for. Really, really yummy. And low fat too I'll be bound. Good for your figure."

"No thank you."

"The nougat then," Blond persisted in desperation. "Everybody likes nougat."

"I don't."

Blond knew when to stop flogging a dead horse and what he was now faced with was a horse deader than Shergar. "As you wish," he said. He waited for a moment or two, so as not to arouse suspicion, then said: "Blast, would you believe it, I bought cigarettes and now I find I've run out of matches! Shan't be long."

Thankfully the Turkish Delight Blond had dropped down the lavatory pan was still there. He quickly fished it out and dried it off with his handkerchief, especially made for him by Gartons of Norwich. Fortunately there was enough of the Mickey Finn left in the syringe to doctor the Turkish Delight. After doing this Blond placed the chocolate back in its allotted slot in the box of Black Magic, had another pee, then made his way back to reception.

"You'll be pleased to learn I gave the shopkeeper a flea in his ear for selling boxes of Black Magic minus the Turkish Delight," Blond announced, as he approached the secretary's desk opening the box of chocolates once more. "He apologised profusely and replaced the box with this box. In which there most certainly is a Turkish Delight," he concluded, pointing to it.

On learning that Blond had gone to such trouble the secretary was pleasantly surprised; but then she wasn't aware that the chocolate had just spent the last five minutes down the lavatory. She smiled. "You shouldn't have bothered."

"No bother."

"Well then," she said, and took the Turkish Delight from the box and popped it into her mouth.

Five seconds later she was spark out, dead to the world, her head slumped on the desk. Blond tidied her up a little so that she looked like a secretary who was just snatching forty winks rather than one who had been shot and left for dead, then made for Goldnojaws' office.

Once inside the office Blond's first priority was a closer look at the giant wall map of Stockport. He immediately saw that there were now more than twice the number of flags stuck in it than on his previous visit.

The last time Blond had been in the office all the flags had been green. Now, although predominately green, some of the flags were red. One was gold. Blond pondered over the choice of colours. Red for danger? Green for go? Gold for....Goldnojaws?

Blond didn't know how much time he would have alone in the office so he took out his pen camera, especially made for him by Leica of Switzerland, and quickly took a photograph of the map. Next he took a photo of the large desk with the pictures of the crane fly and locust on the wall behind it.

Blond wondered at the significance of the size of the desk. It would have been a large desk even for a normal-sized man but for a dwarf it was ridiculously large. This did not surprise him. People short in stature habitually have a penchant for big things, it gives them a feeling of importance, much like the importance felt by city dwellers who drive around in unnecessary Range Rovers and other oversized 4X4s; although it is true to say that such people are just as likely to be as short of brains as they are of height.

Blond then photographed the other walls, then the floor and ceiling, and had just put his camera away and was about to give the map his closer attention when the door opened and Goldnojaws stepped in.

"You!" the dwarf gasped in surprise.

"I've brought the cheque," said Blond, keeping his cool and reaching into his pocket. "Your secretary was asleep and I didn't want to disturb her so I thought I'd leave it on your desk."

"Then do that," Goldnojaws snapped, quite obviously not best pleased at the intrusion. "Then go."

"As you say, Dr Goldnojaws" said Blond suavely. He put the cheque on the desk. "I'll say goodbye then."

"Goodbye, Mr Blond."

Blond started. Had Goldenjaws rumbled him or had he simply mispronounced his name? He corrected the dwarf. "Bland. My name is Bland, Dr Goldnojaws."

Goldnojaws fixed him with an icy stare. "Your name is Blond." He was very sure of himself. "James Blond, Secret Agent SA-Seven."

Blond could see there was nothing to be gained by his denying it. "When did you find out?"

Goldnojaws sneered. "I have known all along, Mr Blond. It is I who caused you to be here in the first place. I knew that my activities and the names of Goldnojaws and BloJob would draw you here to Stockport."

Blond reflected that he had been right when he had expressed those very fears to Maddox. "You admit your names are aliases then?"

Goldnojaws laughed. "But of course."

"And why would you want to draw me here, Dr Goldnojaws? Or whatever your name is."

"Why to belittle you of course, Mr Blond. To observe your crude attempts to bring me to what you call justice. To be amused by your futile attempts to stop me from dominating Stockport...... and with it the world! Now get out of my sight."

Blond looked down at Goldnojaws. Nothing he could do or say could improve the current situation. But he was determined that the dwarf wouldn't have things all his own way. He knew immediately what he could do to redress the balance. He quickly walked up to Goldnojaws, bent over, took him by the shoulders, picked him up and set him down on the desk.

Goldnojaws screamed blue murder. "Bastard! Fucking cunt" he snarled, his face contorted with rage. He shook his fist at Blond. "You'll pay for this, Blond. With your life!"

Blond walked casually to the door. Before leaving the office he turned and regarded Goldnojaws, still comically stood on his desk. "Oh and by the way," he said, the beginnings of a grin appearing at the corners of his mouth, "Regarding your sexual appetite for big women. Believe me Goldnojaws, a man such as yourself would be far better off in a gnome."

Blond's grin broadened as he turned to leave. Who needed a scriptwriter?

CHAPTER THIRTEEN

A SOCIAL EVENING

Earlier that morning, after breakfasting on heavily boiled eggs, toast and coffee, Blond had made a close study of the photographs he'd taken in Goldnojaws' office the previous day. He had blown up the large photograph of Stockport on the wall of Goldnojaws' office and it was now a similar-sized image projected onto the wall of Blond's hotel room.

As he carefully examined it the secret agent paid particular attention to the location of the flags stuck in the map at various points. There were thirteen flags in all, eight green, four red, one gold. Of the thirteen locations, Blond had already visited the Air Raid Shelters, the Casino Royale and the bowling green at Torkington Park. Each of those locations was flagged green. He had seen, although not visited, another of the locations, the Pyramid building, which was also flagged green. The Air Raid Shelters, the Casino Royale and the Pyramid building were all fairly central, as was the football ground, which was flagged red. The Façade shoe factory was flagged gold - so Blond had almost certainly been right in his assumption that it stood for Goldnojaws.

The other eight locations, which were all parks, were spread around the outskirts of Stockport, forming a rough circle, with the Pyramid building at the centre. An epicentre? A command centre? One of the eight parks was Torkington Park, where Blond had played the game of bowls with Goldnojaws. Five of the parks, including Torkington, were flagged green, the remaining three were flagged red.

Blond's brow furrowed in deep concentration. What did Goldnojaws want with eight parks? Or did he in fact want eight parks? Maybe like Torkington Park it was just the bowling green within the parks that he required? Why were five of the parks flagged green whilst the others were flagged red? And was it by design or chance that the parks formed a rough circle round the perimeter of the town with the pyramid building at its centre?

If the idea wasn't so far-fetched as to be in the realms of fiction it would be easy to imagine a wall connecting the parks, isolating Stockport from the rest of the world. What was it Goldnojaws had said? "....to stop me dominating Stockport, and with it the world." How could dominating Stockport, a humble Cheshire town, also mean world domination? It was all very puzzling.

One other thing on the map was puzzling too. A straight line had been drawn with a black marking pen joining the Air Raid Shelters with the Pyramid building situated approximately a mile to the north east. The River Mersey was close by the Air Raid Shelters but curiously the line was broken at that point, indicating that it had not gone over the river but under it. Why? Having been down the shelters Blond knew they were quite deep, but deeper down than the river? Doubtful. And why the line connecting them with the Pyramid? Was it part of Goldnojaws plan to physically connect the two locations in some way? With an underground road or railway perhaps? If so, why?

Too many conflicting ideas were crowding Blond's head and he decided to put all these questions to which he didn't know the answers on the backburner for the time being.

He began to look at the other photos he'd taken in Goldnojaws' office. He learned nothing at all from the one he'd taken of the floor, apart from the fact that Goldnojaws had terrible taste in carpets, and the photos of the walls revealed little more. Apart from the wall behind the desk with the two blown-up photographs of a crane fly and a locust, one of the walls was bare but for a clock, one contained a chart that graphically documented Façade's range of bespoke shoes, and on the remaining wall were two further photos. One of them was a portrait of Goldnojaws posing in the time-honoured fashion beloved of all businessmen, with his chin resting on the knuckles of one hand, trying to look intelligent. The other was of him being presented to Her Majesty Queen Elizabeth II at some function or other.

Blond wasn't at all surprised that such a thoroughly bad lot as Goldnojaws had been presented to Her Majesty; thousands of criminals and scoundrels must have been presented to the Monarch over the years; and of course she regularly met politicians.

Goldnojaws' interest in crane flies and locusts might merit further investigation Blond mused, although he couldn't for the life of him imagine how they might help someone dominate Stockport, much less the world.

He opened his laptop and employed the Google search engine to find out a little about them in the hope it would offer up a clue. He logged on to the first entry on Google's listings and moments later was reading:-

Crane flies are among the insects which cause the most panic in a bedroom, apart from probably spiders, that is. Attracted by the light, they fly in the window and start to flap against lampshades of the main light or the bedside light. Apart from this they do no harm at all. Crane flies are merely large flies. They do not feed as adults, nor do they bite or sting. The female lays eggs in the ground, where the larvae, often known as 'leatherjackets' because of their tough, leathery skins, feed on vegetation, sometimes causing damage by gnawing at the roots of plants. They normally live in damp earth, and sometimes thatch. The larvae itself causes little damage but if crows or other birds discover them they are a source of food, with consequent damage as the larvae are ripped from the ground. When they hatch out these rather leggy flies, sometimes referred to as Daddy Longlegs, are quite harmless. As adults they do not feed, bite or sting. They are unpopular with gardeners as they will feed on grass roots, destroying lawns. Crane flies only live for a period of twenty four hours. This means that they all have to emerge from the ground at the same time to have even a remote chance of breeding.

Blond digested the information. Was it possible that this innocuous, quite harmless insect was in some way connected to Goldnojaws' plan to dominate Stockport? If it was, whatever he was going to do he would have to be quick about it as apparently they only lived for twenty four hours. No, it was much more probable, as Goldnojaws himself had claimed, that he was merely interested in them, that they were just a hobby. People have far stranger, far less fathomable interests than crane flies; train spotting, line-dancing, watching 'I'm A Celebrity Get Me Out Of Here'. Blond punched the word 'locust' into Google's search box. Maybe it would be more fruitful? A moment or two later he read:-

A locust is a large grasshopper showing pronounced, density-dependent polymorphism, that is, the development of different types of individuals brought about by changes in the size, or numbers, of their population. About a dozen species in the short-horned grasshopper family, Acrididae, have evolved this capacity to change their habits and appearance according to their population density. When populations are sparse the individuals live separate lives and migrate singly at night, like other grasshoppers. As their numbers increase however, they respond to more frequent encounters with one another by becoming more and more gregarious, active, and conspicuous. The swarming and non-swarming forms are known, respectively, as the gregarious and solitarious phases. As more and more of the gregarious types appear, characterized by their restless movement, migratory swarms build up. Once started, a locust plague may last for several years while generations of the swarms can overrun entire regions and small countries. Because of their mobility and devastating effects on crops, swarming locusts are greatly feared and difficult to control. The most famous species, the desert locust, Schistocerca gregaria, roams over central and North Africa, the Middle East and India. The locust, which has a lifespan of from a few days to several months, can only survive in hot countries.

Blond sat back in his chair thoughtfully. This was more interesting. More threatening. He could see immediately that if the wrong man could in some way control a swarm of locusts, which apparently had the power to decimate a region or a whole country at the drop of a hat, then that man would be holding very strong cards indeed. But first he would have to be able to control a swarm of locusts. Assuming that he could get hold of such a thing in the first place. A plague of locusts wasn't the sort of thing you could buy, like a football club or a casino or a shoe factory. Besides, this was Stockport, not Ethiopia, and locusts could only survive in hot countries. Even if Goldnojaws were able to acquire a swarm of locusts they would perish before they'd even had the chance to nibble on their first tomato or Brussels sprout in some Stockport allotment. No, Blond decided finally, like the crane fly the locust was probably just an interest of Goldnojaws.

Blond went back to the map of Stockport. Putting it on the back burner hadn't worked this time for it still remained as large an enigma as it had previously. He put it back on the front burner and proceeded to pace the floor; maybe this aid to concentration would help. What did it all mean for God's sake? All the purchases made by Goldnojaws? The green and red flags? The line drawn from the Air Raid shelters to the Pyramid? There was only one thing for it; he would have to view all the locations on the ground, in situ. It just might help to trigger something off.

The decision having been made he took out his silver hip flask, poured into its cap a generous measure of the 80 proof brandy especially made for him by Sir Osis of the Liver - as Blond had jokingly named his brandy importer - and downed it in one. The fiery brew hit the back of his throat. That was better. Much better. Blond was not normally a morning drinker but in this case he made an exception; there was a long day ahead of him and he really felt the need.

*

Visiting all thirteen of the locations on the map was taking Blond quite a bit longer than he had bargained for. The reason was his prostate gland; for after he had visited the first of the parks on his list he had had to go to the toilet.

As is now the case with almost all towns and cities in England public conveniences are so very few and far between as to be almost non-existent. If they were animals or birds or some lower life form such as the natterjack toad they would by now have been classed as an endangered species and something done about it. A hundred years ago public lavatories were much more plentiful, the bulk of them having been built in Victorian times, many of them so ornate and palatial both inside and out that it almost seemed a shame to relieve oneself in them. Nowadays chance would be a fine thing. Never mind an ornate peeing palace, a wooden shed would do. A large cardboard box with a bucket in it? Bring it on. But as the population of the country has increased so has its stock of public conveniences decreased in inverse proportion, as though anyone born after 1900 has no need to relieve him or her self several times a day.

The answer of course, when one needs to spend a penny, is to nip into a public house and use their facilities, and that is what most people do, Blond included. Blond's problem however, unlike all but a few of his fellow countrymen, was that his inherent sense of fair play didn't allow him to use a pub's toilet facilities without first buying a drink.

Therefore it wasn't very long after he'd stopped at one pub for a pee before he'd had to stop at another pub for another pee, the drink he'd had at the first pub by then having found its way to his bladder. This vicious circle ensured that after Blond had visited three of the locations on his list he had also visited three pubs for a drink and a pee, and at the rate he was going the job was going to take forever. Plus the fact that another drink might put him over the drink driving limit, putting his mission in jeopardy should he be pulled in by the police and breathalysed. He knew that he couldn't let things continue in this way or the day would simply disintegrate without him bringing Goldnojaws anywhere nearer to book. He considered his options, then taking the line that if Maddox could refer to himself as M then James Blond could bugger about with names too. So at the next pub he was forced to call at, the Grey Mare Inn, he walked straight up to the bar and announced to the landlord: "My name is Bond. James Bond. Please can I use your toilet?"

The landlord gaped at Blond in disbelief. "James Bond? You mean *the* James Bond? Double-O-Seven?"

"The same. Can I use ....?"

But the landlord was already intent on spreading the good news - Britain's leading secret agent didn't drop into your pub every day of the week! He called out to the only other person in the pub, a man seated at a table in the corner of the bar making out a bet with the assistance of the Daily Mirror's racing page, "Hoy, Arthur." He proudly indicated Blond. "Guess who this is?"

Arthur scowled, clearly annoyed at being dragged away from his equine deliberations. "Ticker, him with the clock up his arse. How the hell should I know who it is?"

The landlord chose to ignore his lone customer's sarcasm. "James Bond," he announced, like the toastmaster at the London Guildhall announcing some important dignitary. "Only James bloody Bond, that's all."

Arthur temporarily forgot all about the odds of Emily's Cottage winning the two-thirty at Wincanton that afternoon. "James Bond?" he exclaimed, with a huge smile. "Well I'll go to our house!"

Blond, unaware that this quaint northern expression meant 'Well, what a surprise!' was himself surprised when Arthur, far from going to his house, got up and joined him at the bar. He now looked at Blond closely, removed his glasses, took out a grimy-looking handkerchief and polished the lenses with it, replaced the glasses, peered again at Blond and said: "You're not James Bond. I've seen James Bond at the pictures, he's a blonde bloke now."

Blond kept his cool. "That's the old James Bond. I'm the new one. I'm on location here, it's my first Bond movie, due to be released early next year."

"What's it called?"

Blond thought quickly. "It's a sequel to 'The World Is Not Enough' - 'Stockport Is Too Much'."

"Stockport Is Too Much? It's about Stockport?" The landlord was delighted at this town boosting news.

"Well I'll go to our house," said Arthur, again not going to his house, but instead taking Blond's hand in his own and pumping it. "What are you having Bondy? On me."

Blond didn't care for the way events were developing. The situation would have to be nipped in the bud immediately. He didn't like lying but sometimes there was nothing else for it. He said: "Thanks all the same but I don't drink."

"Bollocks. A pint of bitter for James Bond, Jack," said Arthur to the landlord. Then added, with a twinkle, "Shaken not stirred."

"He's got it," said the landlord, reaching for one of the row of pint pots hung by their handles above the bar.

Blond was aware that he was going to have to play things carefully. He didn't want to drink any more than he already had as it would inevitably pile up more problems later on, but as he hadn't yet relieved himself he couldn't risk insulting the landlord and Arthur and upsetting them.

He had already observed a door marked 'Gents' on the way to the bar, near to the pub's entrance. He came to a decision. He would make use of the toilet facilities then make a run for it whilst they weren't looking. The ploy devised he smiled disarmingly at Arthur and said: "Why thank you very much Arthur for your kind offer, I don't mind if I do. But first I have to go to the toilet."

"Well even James Bond has to piss I suppose," said Arthur.

And a lot more frequently than you might imagine, thought Blond, as he turned and headed gratefully for the gents.

Inside the convenience, two minutes later, after having relieved himself, Blond eased open the door a few inches and peered out through the crack. The landlord was still at the bar but there was no sign of Arthur. Damn! Where had he disappeared to? Blond opened the door a little farther the better to see. Arthur pulled it open all the way. In his hand he was holding a foaming pint of bitter. He thrust it at Blond. "There you are Bondy," he smiled, "We was beginning to think you'd got lost."

His heart sinking, Blond breathed a sigh of resignation, took the glass of beer and followed Arthur back to the bar. Seeing them the landlord raised his glass and said to Blond: "Here's to your very good health then, Double-O-Seven."

Arthur raised his glass. "To James Bond."

They touched glasses and drank. Blond found the beer to be excellent, Theakston's Old Peculier. In different circumstances he might have enjoyed it. However he had a job of work to do and his only thought was to down the brew as quickly as possible and get the hell out of it.

"My word, you had a thirst on," said the landlord, as Blond drained his glass in one draught and put it down on the bar. He wrapped his hand round it. "Let me fill you up."

Blond protested. "No. No really, I must be off now."

"Bollocks," said the landlord, confirming to Blond that the epithet 'bollocks' apparently meant 'I don't believe you' in Stockport. "I won't hear a word of it," the publican went on. "We won't hear of it will we Arthur. It's not every day James Bond steps into your pub."

"Not every day," agreed Arthur.

While they were drinking their next pint they were joined by another regular, Big David. When Big David was told he was in the company of James Bond he was even more impressed than Arthur and the landlord had been, and despite Blond's protests ordered pints all round.

"Do you mind if I ask you something personal?" Big David said to Blond, after sampling his beer, wiping the foam from his lips and giving it a nod of approval. "Because I've always wondered."

Under normal circumstances Blond, at the risk of being thought of as cold or even worse, stuck-up, would have turned down Big David's request without even considering it. His business was his own business and Secret Service business was nobody's business. Full stop. For all he knew, and although extremely unlikely, the present company might be Russian spies. One could never be absolutely certain in the spy game. However, now fortified with two and a half pints of Old Peculier along with the brandy he'd already had before setting out, plus the two halves of mild he'd had at the previous two pubs, his inhibitions were now lowered by a significant degree, his tongue a little looser. Whatever caution remained was now thrown to the winds. "But of course, Big David," he smiled.

Big David was a little tentative. It was a delicate subject he was about to broach. "Well how many women have you....well, you know....have you....you know."

The landlord was much less tentative. "Shagged. He means how many women have you shagged."

Well at the last count three less than I would have liked to have shagged, thought Blond, but said: "Six hundred."

The landlord's mouth gaped open in a mixture of awe, disbelief and envy. "Six hundred?" It was a figure more than he could contemplate. "Fuck me!"

"Get your trousers down then," said Blond, with a grin.

This rejoinder brought peals of laughter from Arthur, Big David and the landlord, although the landlord's laughter was a little more subdued than that of the others as he wasn't at all sure Blond didn't mean it. When the laughter died down Big David said, very impressed: "Some going, that. Six hundred."

Arthur, although equally impressed, wanted to move the conversation on to another aspect of life in the Secret Service. "And how many men have you killed?" he asked, eagerly.

Blond thought for a moment. "Around thirty." Then added, to assure his drinking partners that he took no glory in killing, that it was simply a job of work, something that had to be done for the good of the country and then forgotten about, "But I didn't of course enjoy killing any of them."

"No," said the landlord, catching the seriousness of Blond's tone, and in turn becoming serious himself. "No, I don't think I would like to have killed thirty men either."

"Nor me," agreed Big David.

"Me neither," said Arthur. He paused in thought for a moment before continuing. "Mind you I wouldn't mind having to kill thirty men if it meant I could fuck six hundred women."

The four of them roared with laughter at this, although Arthur not as loud as the others as he'd meant it.

"I think that calls for another drink." proposed the landlord, and said to Blond: "Your round."

Blond, although anxious to stand his corner, tried to get away with just buying drinks for his three new friends and going on his way before the day was ruined completely. But the company wouldn't hear of it, do you mind mate, do you want to cause offence, are you having a laugh, so he had to buy a pint for himself too. Halfway down his newly charged glass Blond was glad he'd decided to stay, for the germ of an idea had begun to work its way into his consciousness.

Mention of his six hundred conquests had reminded him that he was no longer making any conquests at all and wouldn't be making any ever again unless he could get over the barrier of first discerning whether or not the proposed target of his affections was or was not having her period. He also felt that it would be almost impossible for him to go through the embarrassment of being turned down again. Nor did he much fancy asking another woman if she was having her period if his experience at the hands of Gloria Snockers was anything to go by. Perhaps one or other of the landlord, Arthur or Big David might know how to get over that tricky obstacle? He took the bull by the horns. "By the way," he said, sounding as casual about it as he could, "The six hundred women I've slept with. The strangest thing is that not one of them was having her period when I propositioned her."

"No?" said Arthur, in disbelief.

"Not a single one."

"Amazing," said Big David.

"You lucky bugger," said Arthur. "About half of 'em what I tapped up were. Or they said they were."

The landlord was less impressed, in fact not at all. "Well you'd know, wouldn't you," he said, matter of fact.

"Know?" said Blond.

"Yes. I mean you wouldn't have propositioned them in the first place if you knew they were having their period, would you. And you'd know if they were having their period."

Blond could scarcely believe it had been so easy. He had entertained hopes, true, but they had been fond hopes, hopes of lottery jackpot-winning proportions. And yet right here was this man, this wonderful man, this marvellous publican, who knew the answer. Just like that.

He could scarcely bring himself to ask the question. "How?"

"How what?"

"How would I know if she was having her period?"

"Well she'd have sore nipples, wouldn't she."

Blond, although accepting that this may very well be the case, sore nipples being part and parcel of the baggage of menstruation, immediately saw a snag. He raised it with the landlord without delay. "And how do you know if she has sore nipples?"

"Well you flick them, don't you." The landlord flicked an imaginary nipple with finger and thumb. "And if she winces, she has."

Blond, Arthur and Big David looked at the landlord with disbelief. The landlord, seeing it writ in their faces, defended his method. "Well it works with the wife."

Blond was crestfallen. The landlord's method of menstruation detection might very well work for him, with his wife of some standing and the familiarity that marriage brings with it, but he couldn't see it being of much use to his own cause, feeling in his water that flicking a potential girlfriend's nipples to see if she winced would in all probability bring forth an even more savage response than if he were to ask her if she was having her period.

Fortunately there was now another pint of Old Peculier in front of him in which to drown his sorrows, Arthur having taken advantage of the lull in the conversation to re-order the round.

The late afternoon quickly became the early evening. Another dozen or so people had entered the Grey Mare Inn in their ones and twos. All of them had been introduced to Blond. All of them had wanted to buy him a drink and wouldn't take no for an answer. Blond began to warm to these people of Stockport. They were friendly, uncomplicated people. Simple people, in the straightforward sense of the word. All of them. The landlord, Arthur, Big David, all the other people who'd come into the pub; Peter, Ivor and Nigel, who had befriended him at the bowling green and had willingly offered their advice when he'd asked for it and asked for nothing in return; Mrs Snockers, who had fed him royally on toad-in-the-hole and mushy peas, and her lovely daughter Gloria, who although unable to supply him with sex had generously and of her own free will given him an unforgettable glimpse of the most wonderful breasts he had ever seen or hoped to see. And as far as Maddock's claim that the women of Stockport were ugly was concerned were not the aforementioned Miss Snockers and the delightful Divine Bottom two of the most beautiful young women he had ever met? Who did this Dr Goldnojaws think he was, wanting to dominate their town? Blond would show him! SA-Seven would show the dastardly Dr Goldnojaws whether he would dominate the lovely people of Stockport!

But not just yet, he had another pint coming.

And so the evening wore on. And despite switching to halves around seven-o-clock Blond had drunk twelve pints of Theakston's Old Peculier by the time the landlord and Big David carried him out of the Grey Mare Inn feet first and bundled him into a taxi with instructions to the driver to deliver him safely to the Cheshire Towers Hotel.

He slept every inch of the way.

CHAPTER FOURTEEN

A HELPING HAND

Blond slept all the next day too, save for the time he'd had to get out of bed to take some paracetemol to help stem his throbbing headache, the time he'd had to get out of bed to drink about three pints of water to quell his raging thirst, and the six times he'd had to get out of bed to go to the lavatory for a pee because he'd drunk the three pints of water. It was vicious circle time again. And if the name Old Peculier which Theakston's had given to their brew was meant to be portentous the brewery was not wrong because Blond felt very old and extremely peculiar all day. But by the following morning he was comparatively fit and well again, and ready to continue the task he'd set himself two days previously. However it might be a little easier to accomplish now, as since then he'd had a brainwave that would render the necessity of having to go into public houses to relieve himself a thing of the past.

The secret agent had already visited three of Stockport's parks, Vernon Park, Bredbury Park and North Reddish Park on his previous sortie. He had discovered that a wooden fence, a replica of the one being built at Torkington Park, had already been completed at Vernon Park. At Bredbury Park there had been no such fence. There was also a completed fence at North Reddish Park. Continuing the chain of parks that formed a rough circle within the boundaries of Stockport Blond now made for South Reddish Park. On arriving there he found that, as with Bredbury Park, there was no fence encircling the bowling green.

Before continuing to Heaton Moor Park, the next link in the chain, Blond took time to evaluate the facts he had gathered thus far. Torkington Park had definitely been taken over by Goldnojaws and had a fence surrounding the bowling green. It was flagged green. Vernon Park also had a fence round the bowling green, but was flagged red. North Reddish Park had a fence round it and it too was flagged red. South Reddish Park didn't have a fence and was flagged green. Blond would have expected all the parks with a fence round their bowling green to be flagged green and the others red, or vice versa, but clearly this wasn't the case. He shook his head, completely at a loss. There was neither rhyme nor reason to the pattern so far as he could make out. He shrugged, got back in the Lada and headed for Heaton Moor Park. Maybe that park would offer up a clue?

Whilst on the way there he felt the need to relieve himself. A piece of cake, no longer a problem, he was almost looking forward to it. He turned off the main road into a quiet side street and pulled up. As he got out of the car he had a quick look around. Good, nobody was about. He went round to the back of the Lada, opened the boot, took out the five gallon plastic jerry can he'd purchased at a garage earlier that morning and unscrewed the cap. His practised eyes searched the street once more. No one was coming in either direction. So, standing as close to the back of the Lada as he could and using the boot lid as a shield, he unzipped his fly and inserted his penis into the neck of the jerry can.

He didn't start to urinate immediately. It doesn't work like that when you have a prostate gland problem, and no one was more aware of this than Blond. You have to wait for the pee to come, which it always does, but in its own good time. Even though you might be dying for a pee. The wait can be anything from ten seconds to ten minutes.

Blond had learned from experience that the sound of running water helped to start him off, so when he was in a toilet he always flushed the lavatory and this usually did the trick. However this was Fieldacre Road, Heaton Moor, a street whose pavements had a dozen or so lampposts, several trees, four telegraph poles, eight manhole covers, a post-box and a corner shop, but unfortunately no lavatories.

Blond's contingency plan, for times such as this when no lavatory to flush was available, was to picture in his mind's eye a cascading waterfall. Blond had a vivid imagination and this ploy usually did the trick within thirty seconds or so. It did the trick this time, and twenty seconds after he'd started imagining the Niagara Falls in full flow, eyes tightly closed to aid concentration, Blond began peeing into the jerry can - at exactly the same moment that the Lada began to pull away from him, hijacked by an unseen joy-rider.

If it is difficult for a man who has a prostate gland problem to start urinating then it is even more difficult for him to stop once he's started. Thus when the Lada was fast disappearing into the distance Blond was still holding the jerry can and urinating freely into it when a woman happened to come walking down the street towards him. On seeing Blond, and in particular observing what he was doing, the woman quickly averted her eyes in disgust and quickened her pace.

Not so the two teenage schoolgirls who now came down the street arm in arm. On seeing Blond, and with a broad smile, one of the girls nudged the other to draw her attention to him, then they both had a good giggle about it before the second girl took out her mobile phone and took a photograph of him. As the two went merrily on their way, pausing only to shout "Perv" and "Weirdo" over their shoulders, the young minx who had taken the photo punched the keys on her mobile and in an instant the photo of Blond in mid pee was winging its way through cyberspace to all her friends. Blond wished the earth would open up and swallow him.

He eventually managed to stop the Niagara of urine. But unfortunately not before a police patrol car had screeched to a halt on the opposite side of the road. A police constable burst out of the car as though he had just spotted Osama bin Laden giving Lord Lucan a piggy back and there was a million pounds reward for the capture of each, and along with it the bonus of immediate promotion to Chief Superintendent and a night out with Cameron Diaz. Approaching Blond he leered in the way that only policemen can and said: "And what do you think you're doing, Sunshine?"

Blond swallowed. He was almost lost for words. He managed to mumble an embarrassed "Sorry officer, no offence meant" and made to remove his penis from the jerry can.

The policeman held out the flat of his upraised hand as though Blond were an oncoming juggernaut rather than a stationary urinator and barked: "Hold it." Then, without undue haste, now that he had the law breaker safely captured and under control, he took out a notebook and pencil, methodically licked the point of the pencil and stood with it poised over the notebook. "Name?"

"Blond. James Blond."

"James Blond?"

"Yes."

The constable eyed him suspiciously. "Blond?"

"Yes."

"What do you do for a living?"

"I'm a secret agent."

"Fuck off."

"No, really. My name is James Blond."

"Yes and I'm Donald Duck." The policeman jerked his head towards the car. "Get in the back."

Blond protested. "Please. I really am a secret agent named James Blond."

The constable, more suspicious than a milk bill, looked Blond up and down. He moved as close to him as the jerry can would allow and squinted at his face more closely. Blond tried him with a friendly smile. After a moment the constable smiled back. Blond, taking this as a sign that his adversary was becoming less hostile towards him bucked up a little. However he very quickly bucked back down again when the constable said: "I'm sure I've seen an identikit picture of you recently." Then, sure now, the policeman's face lit up. "I have! You're the suspect we want to interview in connection with an incident in the gents toilet at the Tesco Superstore the other day, aren't you!"

Blond gulped. "No. No of course not. I'm James Blond, a secret agent. As I keep telling you."

The policeman sneered. "Prove it then."

"That could prove to be a mite difficult, stood here as I am with my dick in a jerry can," said Blond, not unreasonably. "But if you'll allow me to put it down for a moment?"

"Go on then." The constable patted the baton hanging from his belt. "But no funny business, or…." He tapped the baton meaningfully.

His hands free Blond quickly put his penis back into his trousers, first things first, then established his credentials. His name and photo on his Secret Service ID card soon convinced the policeman. Blond then told him exactly why he was in Stockport, filled him in with his progress so far, and explained what he was currently doing and how it had been curtailed by the theft of his car.

The policeman nodded towards his patrol car. "Get in the back," he said once again, but this time it wasn't a snarled command but the polite request of someone who saw the possibility of a little reflected glory heading his way.

*

With the constable acting as his chauffeur, the officer's local knowledge of the layout of Stockport as well as his patrol car coming in very handy, Blond's task was all done and dusted three hours later. And with only two pit stops to relieve himself; once at the policeman's home, which happened to be within striking distance of one of the parks they'd visited, and once behind the police car, the policeman this time turning a blind eye to the misdemeanour whilst keeping his other eye open for passers-by.

Having visited all the places indicated on the map that had a flag stuck in them, apart from Façade, Blond had now established that four of the eight parks had fences round their bowling greens, and that there was nothing out of the ordinary going on at the Stockport County football ground, or at least so far as he could determine. There was a hell of a lot out of the ordinary going on at the Pyramid building however.

The scene which greeted Blond on his arrival outside the hundred and fifty feet high glass structure was an absolute hive of activity. Workmen in hard hats were emerging from the interior of the Pyramid carrying doors, floorboards, sections of dividing walls, floor coverings, strip lights, ceiling panels, in fact everything that comprises the interior of an office block, and throwing them on a large heap outside the main entrance. Fork lift trucks loaded with steel girders and sections of floors and ceilings were adding to the heap. In turn the huge buckets of two JCBs were making inroads into the heap and depositing their loads onto large flatbed lorries which were transporting the detritus away.

Blond buttonholed the site foreman and asked him what was going on.

"We're gutting the place," the foreman replied. "Ripping the entire insides out."

"Everything?"

"The lot. All fifteen floors."

Blond wondered why Goldnojaws would buy such a prestigious building and then destroy the entire interior. He asked the foreman if he knew what function the building would fulfil in the future.

The foreman shrugged. "Search me. But when we've emptied it it'll be the world's biggest greenhouse, that's for sure."

Blond left the workers at the Pyramid to their labours and moved on to his last port of call, the Façade factory. On arriving there he asked the policeman to wait. He then walked the whole length of the building, taking his time about it, studying it from every angle, in the hope it might enable him to put his finger on what it was that was wrong with it, that something might click into place.

Seeing the factory again reminded him of Professor Gonzalez. He still hadn't figured out where he fitted into all this. The last time Blond had come up against the brilliant bio chemist he had been breeding giant rats, so whatever he was doing in the shoe factory it certainly wasn't anything to do with shoes, unless Goldnojaws was planning to make shoes big enough to house the Old Woman who Lived in a Shoe, or perhaps adding seven league boots to Façade's footwear catalogue.

Blond reached the far end of the Façade building. He looked back down the length of it. And then completely out of the blue it hit him. It was the windows! At the far end of the factory they were blacked out, as they had been on his previous two visits. But when he had been in the factory, looking down onto the factory floor, all the windows had been transparent. Which meant that there must be an interior wall separating the part of the building with the blacked out windows from the main factory floor. And I bet I know who works behind that wall, Blond thought. Our old friend Professor Gonzalez.

Blond knew it was paramount that he somehow got inside the factory, to see firsthand exactly what was going on in there, and the sooner the better. For something was going on, he was now certain. Or why the blacked out windows?

He looked at his watch. Four-o-clock. The factory finished for the day at five, it went dark about two hours later, around seven. But he would wait until much later than that. This was a job for the night.

CHAPTER FIFTEEN

GOLDNOJAWSUS GONZALIDAE

Five minutes before midnight found Blond back outside Façade. As he looked around once again to double-check if there was anyone in the vicinity half his mind was already wondering what he would discover once he was inside the factory. It could be almost anything. Well he was ready for it no matter what it was.

He recalled previous adversaries, villains who had wished to take over the world, and the methods they had employed to achieve their crazed ambitions; Sir Peregrine Gross, whose plan it had been to level ten square miles of central London with a fleet of atomic bulldozers, and along with it over three million of the capital's populace; Petrolhead, who sought world domination by acquiring all the world's supply of oil and assassinating Jeremy Clarkson; Dr Zog, who sought the same ends with his giant rats; the fiendish Baby Big Brother, who planned to render the entire world brain dead by taking over the world's television stations and feeding the viewing public with wall-to-wall reality programmes, and whose influence remains with us to this day; and, most recently, Singh Singh, whose plan to add a highly concentrated laxative to the world's supply of curry ingredients had had the entire planet shitting itself, both literally and metaphorically, before Blond had finally scuppered the Indian's scheme; and many, many more.

What was it about these power-hungry fiends who appeared with certain regularity that they should want to rule the whole world? Blond would never know, as a law-abiding citizen it was beyond his comprehension; but what he did know was that as long as they kept crawling out from under their rocks he would be there to foil their ambitions, or die in the effort.

On his first visit to Façade Blond had automatically noted the positions of the burglar alarms. They were of a relatively unsophisticated type and would not have detained an average burglar for very long, far less James Blond. However there was a much simpler and entirely risk free way of breaking into the factory, and bravado is never an option when safety is a certainty in the world of the Secret Service, despite what fiction writers of this genre would have the reading public believe.

Blond had noted that the stone sills of the large quartered windows were only two feet above the level of the pavement, each section of window measuring about three feet by two, easily large enough for a man to climb though once the glazing had been removed.

After leaving the Façade factory hours earlier, and before dismissing the policeman and thanking him for his invaluable assistance, Blond had called in at a plumbers' merchants to purchase a lavatory plunger and a glass cutter; then at a grocers he had bought a can of Coca-Cola. Now putting them to good effect he opened the can of Coca-Cola, wetted the rubber suction cup on the end of the plunger with some of the contents and threw the rest away (the concoction had been purchased for its sticky properties, not for human consumption; Blond had once tried drinking Coca-Cola and had too much respect for his stomach to ever risk it again). He then stuck the plunger firmly to the window, cut round the edge of the pane of glass with the glass cutter, and carefully removed the glass from the window frame. Moments later he was inside the Façade factory.

Due to all the windows in this section of the building having been blacked out it was virtually pitch black inside. Blond took out his pencil torch and snapped it on. He played its intense, narrow beam around the room. He was in some sort of laboratory. Given the involvement of Professor Gonzalez in Goldnojaws' plans this came as no surprise to Blond. He aimed the torch at his immediate surroundings. He was at the end of a long row of what were maybe packing cases judging from their rectangular shape, each one covered by a dustsheet.

He took hold of a corner of the first of the dustsheets, carefully pulled it aside and let it drop to the floor. Underneath was not the expected packing case but a glass tank measuring about three feet by two feet by two feet high. Blond directed the torch at the interior of the tank. Inside was the largest crane fly he had ever seen, at least five times the size of a regular crane fly, its dimensions more akin to those of a large dragonfly. Obviously dead, it was mounted on a small plinth. A plaque on the plinth was inscribed 'Crane Fly Diptera, family Tipulidae, 24 hours old'. Blond was not surprised that the crane fly had been only a day old when it had perished as according to his information this was their life span. The size of the insect was a different matter altogether.

He moved along the row and removed the next dustsheet. Underneath was a similar-sized glass tank. Inside was another dead insect about the same size as the one in the first tank, but differing in shape and colour. The plaque on the plinth informed him that it was a 'Locust Acrididae, 24 hours old'.

He moved on and removed the next dustsheet. The tank contained a larger crane fly, dead like its predecessors, but this time about the size of a small lobster. The plaque read 'Crane Fly Diptera, family Tipulidae, 48 hours old'.

Blond's brow creased in puzzlement. Forty eight hours old? How could that be? Crane flies were only supposed to live for twenty four hours. Not totally unexpectedly the next tank revealed a similar-sized locust, and, as was the case with the second crane fly, 48 hours old.

Blond moved the couple of yards to the next tank, his logical mind and ordered thought processes telling him he would see there an even larger crane fly, but to his astonishment he removed the dustsheet to reveal a similar–sized insect to the ones in the previous two tanks that wasn't a crane fly or a locust. He bent to inspect the plaque on the plinth. It read: '*Crane/Locust, aka Superlocust Goldnojawsus Gonzalidae, 48 hours old*'.

Blond gasped and the hair stood up on the back of his neck. So this was what Professor Gonzalez was doing for Dr Goldnojaws at Façade! Breeding super-sized mutations of a crane fly and a locust! Blond looked up the row of tanks. There were about twenty in all, each getting progressively larger. He cut to the chase and made his way to the far end of the line.

The end tank was enormous, measuring about ten feet by ten feet square. He had an idea of what he might find in there but even so his jaw dropped visibly when he pulled aside the dustsheet to reveal the fearsome looking creature within. It was fully ten feet long and of such gargantuan proportions that it barely managed to fit into the tank. Its bulbous black eyes, set in a huge head of more than three feet in diameter, although now deathless, seemed to bore into Blond as it looked down on him. Its shell, a light mauve in colour, looked more like the armour plating used in the manufacture of army tanks than a mere carapace.

Blond tore his eyes away from the hideous vision to look at the plaque on the floor - there wasn't room in the tank for a plinth – and read: '*Crane/Locust, aka Superlocust Goldnojawsus Gonzalidae. 2 weeks old. Fully mature*'.

His mind raced. Crane flies were about an inch and a half long at most and lived for only twenty four hours. Locusts could live for longer but were little bigger than crane flies. But now here was a mutant of the two species, and ten feet long! He gave an involuntary shudder. The prospect didn't bear thinking about. Normally a locust couldn't survive the harsh British climate but would that be the case when it was crossed with a crane fly, a native of the British Isles? If it could indeed survive, heaven only knew what havoc and destruction it would wreak. And Goldnojaws could apparently breed these monsters at will!

Blond was wondering what to do next when suddenly every light in the building came on. Dazzled, he put a hand over his eyes to shield them from the glare. When he cautiously took it away he saw through screwed-up eyes, at the other end of the row of tanks, the diminutive figure of Goldnojaws. Blond caught his breath. "You!"

"Welcome, Mr Blond," said Goldnojaws, suaveness personified. He started to walk towards Blond. "I have been expecting you. What took you so long?"

Blond affected casual bravado. "I had more important things to do, Goldnojaws."

The dwarf's top lip curled in a sneer. "You mean it took your third rate brain this long to add two and two together. Even though I allowed you the freedom of my office the other day."

This claim surprised Blond. "Allowed me the freedom of your office?"

"But of course, Mr Blond. Or did you think it was mere coincidence that I returned to my office minutes after you entered it?" His sneer gave way to a gloat. "Much good it will do you."

By this time he had reached Blond. The secret agent looked down at him and said: "If you think for one moment that you'll get away with this Goldnojaws you are sadly mistaken."

The dwarf raised an eyebrow. "Oh? And may I ask who is going to stop me?"

"I am. Or if not me then some other member of the Secret Service."

"Then it will be some other member of the Secret Service. Because it most certainly won't be you, Mr Blond." With that Goldnojaws looked over Blond's shoulder and barked: "BloJob!"

The lights went out for Blond as quickly as they had come on a minute previously as a fearsome blow landed on the back of his head and he collapsed in a sprawling heap at Goldnojaws' feet.

CHAPTER SIXTEEN

BLOJOB

The hazy ceiling above Blond gradually became more distinct and a minute or so later finally stopped spinning. His head now had a large lump on the crown where BloJob had brought the sand-filled sock crashing down on it and was throbbing as though someone had been let loose in it with a jack hammer. Feeling decidedly groggy he looked around him in an effort to find his bearings. Seconds passed before he was back in control of his senses sufficiently enough to recognise Goldnojaws' office and recall his visit to Façade.

He looked down at himself and realised he was lying on the dwarf's large desk. He was bound tightly to it by two thick leather straps that encircled his chest and hips. His arms were secured by rope, tied to each wrist. He surmised that the other end of the rope was attached to the legs of the desk. His own legs were untied, but securing them wasn't necessary as his trousers and underpants, especially made for him by Big Boy of Birmingham, had been pulled down around his ankles, doing away with the necessity of any further restraints. Above and to the left of him the large photographs of the crane fly and the locust looked down at him, as if to mock him. He now knew, much too late, that they weren't blown-up photographs at all but life-sized photographs, and with this realisation all the events prior to his losing consciousness came flooding back into his aching head.

No sooner had this happened than as if on cue the door opened and Goldnojaws stepped in. BloJob was in close attendance. Blond guessed they had probably been watching him, waiting for him to regain consciousness. He steeled himself, fearing the worst. He had been in scrapes like this before, defenceless and at the mercy of a crazed villain, and if he knew anything at all it was that it was now torture time. He speculated as to what form the torture might take. His trousers and underpants being round his ankles didn't augur well.

Goldnojaws marched up to Blond with the air of a man who has just won the battle and knows he is now a racing certainty to go on to win the war. Then he rather spoiled the effect by climbing up onto his desk chair - the only way in which he could look down at Blond – and which he now proceeded to do for a good half minute, enjoying the experience, before finally speaking. When he did his voice was full of loathing, his words coated with venom. "Pick me up and put me on my desk would you Mr Blond?" he spat out. "Well it is you who are now on my desk."

"So it would appear," said Blond laconically, but sounding a lot calmer than he felt.

Goldnojaws raged on. "I'd be far better off in a gnome, would I? Well you would be far better off in a swamp, Mr Blond, in a swamp up to your neck in quicksand and still sinking, or in a cageful of man-eating tigers who hadn't eaten for a week, or indeed anywhere on earth except where you are now, because believe me Mr Blond where you are now is the very worst place you could be." He took a few seconds to calm down before continuing. "And now, is there anything you would like to know, anything you would like me to tell you before you begin your slow, painful journey to death?" Blond said nothing, contenting himself with looking at Goldnojaws with all the contempt he could muster. The dwarf continued. "Perhaps you would like to know exactly how I intend to dominate Stockport, and with it the world, Mr Blond? Perhaps your inadequate mind hasn't yet worked it out?" Blond remained tight-lipped. Goldnojaws grew impatient. "Well, Mr Blond, do you want to know or don't you?"

Blond finally spoke. "I'm sure you're going to tell me Goldnojaws, regardless of whether I wish to know or not."

Blond was aware that if there was one more certainty in the world, along with death and taxes, it was that power-crazed villains bent on world domination would reveal their plans to you once they had captured you and had you at their mercy. It came with the territory; the need to boast about their achievements being so obligatory with crazed despots it wouldn't have been out of place on their CV. Blond had been subjected to it a number of times in the past. As he expected, his sarcasm was completely wasted on Goldnojaws, who now proceeded to regale him with his grand scheme. "As you have seen," the dwarf said, "I have the capability to breed a mutation of the crane fly and the locust. I have named it the superlocust."

"I'll bet that took a lot of thought," Blond said, drily.

Goldnojaws ignored the jibe and carried on. "All I require to breed these creatures is an adequate supply of crane flies. Locusts are easy to come by but crane flies present a problem as they only appear once every year, when they emerge from their chrysalis and live for just a few short hours. Or should I say did live for a few short hours; for now, thanks to my good friend Professor Gonzalez, the crane flies under my control will be able to survive for up to a week. A period of time which is more than enough time for my needs. And once I have a supply of both crane flies and locusts....well, you have already seen what it is now in my power to create from them."

"And once you have some of these monstrosities?"

"Not some, Mr Blond. The collective name for a group of locusts is 'swarm'. Although personally I prefer the expression 'a plague' of locusts, which is entirely appropriate given that not only does plague mean 'epidemic' but when employed as a verb means 'to torment, to cause distress'. Which is what I am going to do to the unfortunate people of Stockport with my plague of superlocusts."

"And torment is all you will be capable of Goldnojaws," Blond scoffed. "Because any torment your superlocusts may be capable of won't be anything like enough to bring the people of Stockport to their knees. The very worst your mutant monstrosities will be able to do is eat all their crops; and correct me if I'm wrong but I don't think Stockport is all that renowned as a crop-growing area."

Goldnojaws bent over, the better to laugh in Blond's face, which he did before saying with incredulity: "Crops? Crops, Mr Blond? My superlocusts will not just eat crops. You underestimate me. Bushes, hedges, trees, cats, dogs, babies, small children, they will devour all these things. And once it has become clear what they can do then the world will be mine for the asking. The governments of the super powers will be lining up to hand me autonomy over them."

Blond's blood ran cold. Could Goldnojaws possibly mean what he had said? Babies and small children? He regarded the dwarf, and now for the first time saw the glint of madness in his eyes, a quality he was well-qualified to recognise, it was something he had seen all too often in the past. Yes, Goldnojaws was capable of carrying out his threat all right.

Blond knew it would serve no purpose trying to reason with the dwarf. He had long since learned that it is impossible to reason with the insane, for the ability to reason is missing from their make-up. All he could do was play for time and hope that something would come up. Before setting out he had informed Maddox of his progress on the assignment thus far, and of his intention to get inside the Façade factory, so help would arrive eventually once he had failed to report in to HQ at the appointed hour and they realised he'd gone missing.

"And when will this far-fetched event take place?" Blond now asked, his will to survive not extending to the abandoning of sarcasm when addressing Goldnojaws.

"In approximately six month's time. Not that you will be around to witness it, Mr Blond. That is when crane flies appear for their very brief spell on earth. And once they do I will have a plentiful supply of them, more than enough for my needs."

"And how will you acquire them?"

"You don't know, Mr Blond?" Goldnojaws sounded like a schoolteacher addressing a particularly slow-on-the-uptake pupil. "You are not even as bright as I thought you were. Which isn't all that bright, I must confess." He spelled it out slowly, for Blond's benefit. "The four bowling greens I own, Mr Blond. The leatherjacket, which is the chrysalis from which the crane fly pupae emerges, thrives in wet, soggy turf. And is it possible to have more wet soggy conditions than those to be found on a bowling green in the north west of England? Especially a bowling green of which I have complete control, and can keep at optimum dampness?" Goldnojaws paused for a moment before going on. "The Air Raid Shelters complex which I have recently acquired will be made much larger, by excavation. Ten thousand square metres of sandstone will be removed, resulting in a single underground area in excess of fifteen thousand square metres. This is where my superlocusts will be bred." He paused for a moment and allowed himself a smirk before continuing. "You will no doubt have noticed on my map a line leading from the Air Raid Shelters to another of my acquisitions, the Pyramid building, connecting the two. This line represents a five metres wide road set within a three metres high tunnel. Once the superlocusts are fully developed they will be shepherded from the Shelters to the Pyramid from where they will be released on Stockport to do their worst."

Blond gasped on learning the scale of Goldnojaws' deadly operation. There was little doubt his plan would work if and when it was effected. "And the football ground and the casino? And the other four bowling greens? How do they fit into your plans?"

"They have already successfully played their part."

"In what way?"

Goldnojaws smiled. "As red herrings, Mr Blond. As were the green and red flags which no doubt confused your feeble brain. Ploys to throw any would be inquisitors off the scent, to confuse them, to have them going round in circles, as you yourself went round in circles before quite literally going round in circles when you visited all the bowling greens on the map."

Blond still found it hard to believe that someone would go to such lengths. "You spent goodness knows how many millions of pounds just to throw me off the scent?"

"You, and any other deluded idiots who might fool themselves into thinking they can stop the inevitable. But of course!"

It didn't make any sense to Blond. "Then why go to the trouble of calling yourself Goldnojaws? Thereby ensuring the Secret Service became suspicious of you and your activities in the first place?"

Goldnojaws grinned. "Because I am a little shit, Mr Blond. Simply that. As you are now about to find out." He turned to BloJob. "He is all yours, BloJob." He turned from Blond dismissively and made for the door.

Rubbing her hands in anticipation BloJob walked over to Blond. She took off her hat, removed the ever present chewing gum from her mouth and stuck it underneath the desk top. She looked down at Blond, her hideous face creased in a smile, then leaning over him took his penis into her mouth and started to suck it. Despite himself Blond became hard immediately.

When as a teenager Blond had first heard of blow jobs he hadn't fancied the idea one little bit. A girl taking a chap's penis in her mouth and blowing, far from being an enjoyable experience, sounded positively dangerous. For one thing, where did the air go? Up your urethra? No, thank you very much, don't like the sound of that at all. He had decided there and then that he never wanted anything to do with blow jobs. No, what he wanted were suck jobs, and plenty of them. A couple of years on he learned that what he had conceived as a suck job was in fact a blow job and promptly joined the queue. Since then, thanks to his glamorous occupation and blond good looks, a deadly combination that had always guaranteed him a never-ending supply of the world's most beautiful women, he had been on the receiving end of literally hundreds of blow jobs, all of them acceptable, most of them very enjoyable, some of them quite superb.

One of the very best had been performed on him by Chantelle de Lyon, whose licking technique was beyond reproach. Equalling her, not as good as Chantelle at licking but absolutely unbeatable at sucking, had been Vicki Violet, in the Petrolhead case. However, and as excellent as those two girls had been, they both failed to reach the standard set by the fellatio performed on him by the wonderful Glynis Gam. Especially after she'd taken her teeth out.

BloJob was something else. Different class. The combined efforts of the three girls previously mentioned paled into insignificance when compared to the blow job now being performed on him by the gigantic Australian. Her mouth, up until then known to Blond only for its coarseness, was the exact opposite when employed in the act of fellatio. It was a mouth of liquid velvet. Warm, soft, liquid velvet, now clamped tightly round his pulsating penis. The whole of his penis.

Blond thought at first that BloJob must have had lessons from Linda Lovelace of Deep Throat fame, but the longer it went on the more he came to realise that in all probability it was BloJob who had given Linda Lovelace lessons, such was her expertise. Blond had had his testicles licked on many occasions but never before at the same time as his penis had been in the girl's mouth.

The performance lasted for over thirty minutes before he finally ejaculated, mercifully, before he burst. BloJob had brought him to the brink at least a dozen times only to withdraw, before starting again, playing him like a musical instrument, bringing him to a crescendo before suddenly breaking off and lapsing into a quiet passage before building up to a crescendo again, and yet again, until mercifully Blond came and the symphony was over.

BloJob withdrew from Blond, swallowed, smiled down at him, rescued her chewing gum from under the desk top, put it in her mouth and started to chew.

Blond looked up at her. "Marry me," he said.

CHAPTER SEVENTEEN

RELIEF

Twenty four hours later the last thing on earth Blond wanted was to be married to BloJob. Betrothal to the Devil himself would have been preferable.

Five minutes after BloJob had fellated Blond she had taken him into her mouth again. Blond became hard again almost at once. This didn't surprise him, he had always been a three times a night man, and don't necessarily rule out a fourth.

The second time had been just as impossibly wonderful as the first, but over much more quickly, five minutes at the most. BloJob had brought him to a climax without all the crescendos; in duration not so much a symphony, more a prelude, but a very enjoyable prelude for all that. It was also, however, a prelude of far worse things to come.

No sooner had BloJob finished than Goldnojaws returned to the room. He was carrying a large hypodermic syringe. He indicated Blond. "Roll up his sleeve," he said to BloJob, all business.

BloJob roughly pushed up the sleeve of Blond's jacket, ripping it in her carelessness. Goldnojaws climbed up on the chair as before and dramatically held up the syringe to the light to check the contents, at the same time making sure Blond got a good look at it, and said: "A little concoction prepared by Professor Gonzalez."

"Don't tell me Goldnojaws, I'm going to grow an enormous cock," said Blond, coolly.

"I'm glad to see you have retained your sense of humour, Mr Blond," said Goldnojaws, as he searched for a plump vein in the crook of Blond's arm. "Hold onto it, enjoy it while you can, for you won't have much of a sense of humour left by the time BloJob and I have finished with you." He found a suitable vein. "This might hurt a little," he warned, before savagely plunging the needle into Blond's arm, thus ensuring that it definitely did hurt, much to the dwarf's amusement.

Blond flinched but managed not to cry out in pain. There was no way he would give Goldnojaws the satisfaction of knowing that he was hurt.

Goldnojaws indicated the syringe as he withdrew the needle. "Highly concentrated Viagra. It would give a eunuch an erection."

Although Goldnojaws' claim for the efficacy of the contents of the syringe was an obvious exaggeration Blond was left in no doubt that it worked because scarcely had BloJob removed her chewing gum and lowered her head over him than he achieved tumescence again.

Over the course of the next eight hours BloJob brought James Blond to a climax no less than forty three times. Each time Blond ejaculated BloJob injected him with another shot of the concentrated Viagra. At the end of the eight hours the secret agent was physically, totally spent.

The fellatio had long since ceased to be an enjoyable experience. Now it had become all but unbearable. BloJob's mouth, although still the quality of liquid velvet, was no longer an instrument of passion but a contrivance of torture. Now each time the Australian brought Blond to a climax she did so as quickly as possible, and without taking the trouble to keep her small pointed teeth out of the way of his penis, a penis that was fast becoming red raw due to the brutal treatment it had received. In fact on a couple of occasions the Australian actually chewed on it for good measure with the result that Blond's wedding tackle took on the appearance of something more suitable for a funeral.

When having sex a man will often turn his mind to something other than the act he is engaged in, in an effort to delay ejaculation. Throughout his ordeal Blond had been employing this technique, but on this occasion not to delay ejaculation but to take his mind off the terrible torture BloJob was visiting upon him. His method was to compile lists. He had already compiled a list of his Ten Most Satisfying Sexual Conquests and his Ten Favourite Golf Courses. Now, upon recalling that one of his ten most satisfying sexual conquests had been on a golf course, in a pot bunker at Royal Birkdale to be precise, he was compiling a list of the ten most unusual locations in which he had had sex. He added the final one, in the Savoy Grill's Dumb Waiter (with a dumb waitress), and turned his attention to the 'Ten Things He Was Most Unlikely To Do'. He started with 'Go To A Coldplay Concert', added 'Read More Than The First Page Of Any Book Written By Tolkien', 'Watch Any TV Programme With The Word 'Celebrity' or 'Dancing' In The Title', 'Embrace Homosexuality', and was about to include 'Embrace Janet Street-Porter' to the list when quite incongruously, especially when considering what he was thinking about at the time, he reached a climax. BloJob, her job done for the time being, mercifully left the room. Blond quickly dismissed Janet Street-Porter from his mind and went to sleep almost immediately.

He had no idea how long he slept but the next thing he was conscious off was being shaken into wakefulness by Goldnojaws. The hulking figure of BloJob was back at the dwarf's side, a hideous grin on her face.

"Wakey wakey, Mr Blond," said Goldnojaws, affecting a cheery tone. Blond peered at him through half-shut bleary eyes. He groaned inwardly. Goldnojaws went on. "What's this SA-Seven? Not bright-eyed and bushy-tailed after all that sleep?" He didn't bother to wait for an answer. "Too bad, because your punishment is about to continue. But first, my story."

This time Blond's groan was audible and even more heartfelt. He had imagined he'd got away with it this time but the dwarf's words informed him otherwise. He might have known, for just as all villains bent on world domination feel it necessary to reveal their plans once they have you at their mercy they also see it as a duty to tell you their life story. As if Blond could care less about Goldnojaws' life when his own life was swiftly ebbing away!

However, looking on the positive side, the relating of Goldnojaws' life story would eat up a little more time, and Blond was well aware that time was a commodity he needed as much of as he could get. More time meant more chance of being rescued from this horrible fate. He therefore feigned interest, or as much interest as he could given his condition. "I'd love to hear your story, Dr Goldnojaws," he croaked. "I'm sure I will find it most interesting."

Goldnojaws began. "My real name is Robert Evans. I was born in Stockport forty two years ago and grew up there. Although not very much, as you can see." He looked pointedly at Blond. "You see, I too have a sense of humour, Mr Blond," he said with a smile, before continuing. "I have always been smaller than my peers, even as a child. All small children are bullied at school and I was no different. Even the small children who the other children bullied used to bully me. The teachers, though not bullying me physically, bullied me mentally, in the sadistic manner that only teachers can, which is far worse. They used to say things to me like 'Sit up, Evans..... oh, you are sitting up'. And if I put my hand up and asked if I could leave the room they would say they thought I had already left it. As a result of all the physical and mental bullying I persistently played truant, to get away from it, and because of this my school work suffered and I left school at the age of fifteen with nothing more than an O-level in woodwork. But, more significantly, an A-level in an abiding hatred of my fellow human beings."

He paused for a moment before carrying on, as if to bestow more importance to the next part of his speech.

"You must understand Mr Blond that this was in an age, and not so very long ago at that, when discrimination against anybody who wasn't perceived as normal was still rife in this country; a time when employers could refuse you even an interview for a job if you were a dwarf, let alone the job itself. Because of this attitude towards me I was on the dole for two whole years after leaving school. Then my luck changed, or so I thought, when I obtained a position as a chimney sweep's assistant; a post I was to leave after less than one morning when I discovered that the chimney sweep was a depraved individual heavily into Charles Dickens who wanted me to climb up the chimneys. It was almost Christmas at the time and on my way home I saw that a local theatre, the now defunct Davenport on Buxton Road, was staging a production of the pantomime Snow White and the Seven Dwarves. Great I thought, what could be more perfect, I'm a dwarf, I will be ideal. So I applied for a job. I was turned down flat. Can you imagine how I felt when that happened to me, Mr Blond? What that did to me? I couldn't even get a job as a fucking dwarf!"

Blond remembered having seen Snow White and the Seven Dwarves when he was a boy but couldn't recall seeing any fucking in it, and to amuse himself wondered idly if the role of the fucking dwarf for which Goldnojaws had applied had been in an adult production of the pantomime that maybe had dispensed with the services of Sleepy and Dopey and replaced them with Shaggy and Gropey.

Goldnojaws voice cut into his thoughts. "Not surprisingly I decided to leave England for good. To emigrate to a country where such considerations as a person's size are of no importance. Do you know what that country was, Mr Blond?"

"Lilliput?"

Blond's quip was spontaneous, but given the hopelessness of his situation even if he'd taken the time to consider the possible repercussions of uttering it he would probably have said it all the same. He need not have worried, Goldnojaws was about to embark on the successful part of his life, his glory years, and he wasn't about to let a cheap shot from a man who was soon about to die delay him.

"Russia, Mr Blond. Soviet Russia. Communism, a system of government where everyone is equal. Or at least equal enough to treat people of restricted growth such as myself as equal." Goldnojaws paused to light a cigarette. Blond resisted the temptation to tell him that smoking might stunt his growth; what would be the point? Goldnojaws blew a smoke ring and watched it dissipate before carrying on. "I immediately found employment in the oilfields of Siberia. The Vankor oil field in the Krasnoyarsk Kray to be precise. Few will put up with the harsh conditions in Siberia, so getting a job there wasn't difficult. I learned to speak the Russian language. It came easy to me; I discovered I had a natural gift for languages, a gift that had remained hidden during my youth, the only language I knew at school being the language of mockery at my dwarfism."

"I was earning top dollar and enjoying the life, hard as it was, but I wanted more. So whenever I wasn't working I studied. I took correspondence courses in geology, chemistry, mathematics, mining, oil production and civil engineering. My doctorate, which is the only genuine part of my alias, is in the sciences, pure and applied. My studies paid off, promotion quickly followed. Soon I was in charge of an oil rig. Five years after leaving England I was plant manager, in charge of the whole operation, the whole shooting match. There was no stopping me now. Do you know what it was that was driving me on, Mr Blond?" Goldnojaws didn't give Blond the chance to reply, even if he'd wanted to, so eager was he to tell the tale. "My hatred of England and all it stands for. My hatred of the people who drove me out of the land of my birth. In particular my hatred of the town of Stockport, where my humiliation was born, took root and flourished."

Goldnojaws dropped the cigarette on the floor and gestured to BloJob to stamp it out before continuing. "This was the era when the Russians discovered they had far more oil than they had previously supposed. The industry was growing fast and there were opportunities waiting to be exploited by the ambitious. No one was more ambitious than me. There were millions upon millions of barrels of oil there for the taking and billions upon billions of roubles to be made by those who helped themselves to those barrels. Some business associates invited me to join with them in creating an oligarchy. Twelve months later I was the head of that oligarchy. In two years it was the fourth biggest oil oligarchy in Russia. However, unlike Roman Abramovitch with his plaything football team, I chose to remain in the background. Because of this very few people have heard of me. However that situation will not last for much longer. Soon the name of Robert Evans alias Goldnojaws will be on the lips of everyone....when I finally take my revenge on Stockport, and through it dominance over the entire world!"

His life story duly delivered Goldnojaws had no further use of Blond. He simply said to BloJob "Continue with the treatment," and turned to leave.

Blond called after him, protesting. "Just what are you trying to achieve with this treatment of me Goldnojaws, Robert Evans, or whatever your name is? You can't kill me by fellatio."

Goldnojaws turned to face him. "Maybe, maybe not, Mr Blond. We will never know. Long before that possible eventuality you will have died through simply having given up the will to live." He turned away from Blond again and left the room. Blond wondered if he would ever see him again.

*

Six hours later Goldnojaws' prophecy that Blond would have given up the will to live had all but been realised. In the time since the dwarf had taken his leave BloJob had brought the sorely abused secret agent to a climax a further eighteen times, and the way Blond was feeling it wouldn't be long before he was in a coffin, especially made for him by Sowerberry and Sons, Funeral Directors, of Swaffam.

Blond looked down at his battered genitals as BloJob refilled the hypodermic syringe yet again. Soon he would be erect yet again and BloJob would be about her terrible business. If anything, given the chance, Blond would have preferred his genitals to have been beaten or kicked rather than receive more of the same treatment from BloJob's terrible mouth, if only for a change from all the sucking that, along with his semen, was drawing the very lifeblood out of him. Not that there was any semen left in him to draw out. It had long since dried up. Now he came but nothing arrived, his testicles drier than a temperance meeting in the Kalahari Desert.

BloJob was about to plunge the hypodermic into Blond's arm yet again. When doing this, and as if she had a fear of the needle herself, she was in the habit of baring her teeth in apprehension, as though it were she herself who was about to be injected. This time as she bared her teeth her chewing gum fell out of her mouth and dropped to the floor.

And Blond had the idea which was to save his life. He wasted no time into putting it into operation.

As BloJob reached in her pocket for a fresh piece of chewing gum Blond said, sharply: "Come on you Australian cow, inject me and be done with your dirty work. Anything as long as you don't take my chewing gum off me."

BloJob peeled the wrapper off the stick of chewing gum. "You blind as well as dumb, shit for brains?" she sneered. "I've got my own chewy, ain't I."

"Good. Then you'll keep your filthy colonial hands off my chewy – which in fact is a superior brand of chewing gum especially made for me by Wrigleys of London."

BloJob cocked her head to one side, interested. "That right? Specially made for you, huh? Must be quite special then."

"It is. And you're not getting any of it, you bitch."

BloJob grinned evilly. "No? We'll soon see about that." With that she took hold of Blond's shoulders and shook him until his teeth rattled. "Where is it, you bush buzzing pommie bastard?"

Blond howled in protest, putting everything into it, as if his life depended on it, which it probably did. "Please! Take anything from me. Take my wallet. Take my watch. Take my life. Take anything but my chewing gum!"

"I don't want your fucking watch and your fucking wallet I want your fucking chewing gum," BloJob snarled, shaking Blond again before slapping him viciously across the mouth with the back of her hand, splitting his bottom lip in the process.

Blond tasted blood. "All right. No more. I know when I'm beaten. It's in my inside pocket."

BloJob felt inside Blond's jacket pocket and took out the stiff upper lip that Postlethwaite had given him a few days earlier. She held it up and squinted at it. "This it?"

Blond nodded. BloJob looked at it more closely. "Funny looking chewing gum. Looks like a lip."

"Yes, that's the idea, you can put it over your lip if you prefer and blow bubbles with it. Personally I prefer to put it in my mouth and chew it."

"So do I," said BloJob, and promptly did just that.

The last thing Blond saw before the blast from the explosion rendered him unconscious was BloJob's head disappearing from her shoulders and her headless body falling stone-like to the ground.

CHAPTER EIGHTEEN

COMA

In the end, in more ways than one, it was a Pakistani index finger that was to give James Blond the opportunity to engage in battle once more with the fiendish Dr Goldnojaws.

If anyone had asked Blond if he was a racialist he would have laughed in their face at the very idea. Perish the thought! All colours and creeds were the same to James Blond, the shade of a person's skin and their religion did not even enter into it; the only thing that mattered to Blond was whether the man or woman in question was good or evil, straight or crooked, for Queen and Country or agin.

Despite this Blond had always felt, indeed had always known, that the British as a race are superior to all foreigners, and that the English were the most superior of all Britons. This fact, set in stone, had been planted in him as a child by his parents Grenville 'Flog the Darkies' Blond, MP. JP. DSO. and his wife The Hon Bunty Blond, nee Browning. It had been nurtured during his education at prep school and later at Eton where he had rubbed shoulders, amongst other parts of his body, with the sons of the British aristocracy, and had blossomed when he had taken up a career in one of the bastions of the British Establishment, MI6.

Therefore on the day the Pakistani doctor put his finger up Blond's bottom it was without any doubt the lowest point in the secret agent's life, and just that little bit lower than if it had it been an English Caucasian who had perpetrated the invasion of his anus. The owner of the offending digit was a Dr Dongh. The 'h' in Dongh was silent; which is more than can be said for Blond a split second after the doctor's index finger disappeared inside his rectum up to the third knuckle.

Despite having been educated at an English public school, an establishment where, along with rugby and cricket, buggery is almost a compulsory sport, Blond had somehow managed to hang on to his anal virginity, and up until his appointment with Dr Dongh had only ever experienced the feeling of things coming down his rectum, in the shape of relatively soft faeces, and never going up, in the shape of a hard, bony finger.

The purpose of the examination of Blond's rectal passage was to determine the condition of his troublesome prostate gland. Whether it was in good order or not there was certainly something not quite as it should be up there because when the tip of Dr Dongh's probing finger touched it the effect on Blond was instant, the outcome alarming. Blond, lying on the doctor's examination couch facing the pale green-painted brick wall, shot forward what would have been eighteen inches if the wall hadn't been only twelve inches away, with the result that he gave himself the most frightful crack on the head. And with it, fortuitously, came the return of his memory.

*

Following the explosion in Goldnojaws' office, and the decapitation and instantaneous demise of BloJob, Blond had remained unconscious, comatose, for the next five months. His body had been found, severely burned but otherwise largely unhurt, in a wheelie-bin in the front garden of an empty boarded-up council house a few hundred yards from the Façade factory. How it had got there no one knew, save for possibly Goldnojaws or someone in his employ, and he wasn't about to tell anybody.

After Blond's disappearance, and before his subsequent discovery a week later by one George Nickerson, a tramp who was looking in the wheelie-bin for anything he could find, Maddox had sent secret agent SA-Nine to Stockport to investigate. Blond's compatriot had interviewed Goldnojaws but the dwarf had claimed that the last time he had seen Mr Bland from L for Leather he had been alive and well.

SA-Nine had stayed on in Stockport in an effort to find out what Goldnojaws was up to but had not been as successful as Blond and after a couple of weeks Maddox had recalled him to HQ. The case had subsequently been put on the back burner, where it still remained.

After he had been found in the wheelie-bin Blond had been taken to Stockport's hospital, Stepping Hill, known to the local populace, since the advent of MRSA and C-difficile, as Step in ill, Step out dead, gallows humour being a particularly popular pastime in Stockport.

No ID had been found on Blond, Goldnojaws having seen to that, but a trace of semen found on the secret agent's Big Boy of Birmingham underpants had provided his DNA. Two days later Blond had been identified.

Just as soon as the doctors at Stepping Hill had diagnosed that Blond, although comatose, was in a stable condition, he had been moved, on the insistence of Maddox, to a private hospital in London. He had remained there, in the same comatose state, until three weeks before his prostate examination at the hands of, or rather the finger of, Dr Dongh.

The doctors assigned to Blond had tried various methods to try to induce the secret agent out of the coma, playing his favourite music (Mozart, Pink Floyd, The Killers), and getting friends to talk to him for long spells about familiar things etcetera, but nothing had worked. Perversely, when all attempts to rouse him had failed, Blond emerged from the coma unheeded, some five months to the day after he had entered it. Maddox had been summoned to his bedside immediately.

"So how are you old chap?" he enquired on his arrival, making an effort to sound bright and breezy in an endeavour to disguise the concern he had for his favourite agent's condition, but failing miserably.

Blond did his best to put his boss's mind at rest. "Just raring to go, sir. Well rested up. In fact more than well rested up and ready to return to duty."

Although delighted with Blond's attitude Maddox was cautious. "Not so fast, James. We must make absolutely sure you are one hundred per cent before we point you in the direction of the world's most infamous criminals once more. Despite the fact that I want you to get to grips with that Goldnojaws character again without any undue delay."

Blond raised a quizzical eyebrow. "Who, sir?"

Maddox jogged Blond's memory. "Goldnojaws. The chap in Stockport we're very interested in."

Blond's eyebrow now reached Roger Moore proportions. "Stockport? I'm afraid I don't understand, sir."

Now it was Maddox' turn to raise an eyebrow. "You do remember going to Stockport?"

Blond shook his head. "I've never been there in my life."

*

It was eventually discovered that Blond had no recollection whatsoever of the four weeks prior to his going into a coma, in fact since the time he was still on the trail of Morientes the Mexican drug trafficker. He had no recollection at all of Goldnojaws and BloJob and his time in Stockport. He could remember nothing of the traumatic trip north in the Lada and the ensuing trouble at Tesco; nothing of his trips to the Air Raid Shelters and the Pyramid building, of Casino Royale and the time spent with Divine Bottom; nothing of his game of bowls with Goldnojaws in Torkington Park and of Mrs Snockers and her lovely daughter Gloria. And nothing of Pisa Vass.

He had excellent recall however of all the other women he had bedded prior to that, and after lying in his hospital bed for a week with nothing to do but 'get better' what Blond needed more than anything was a woman. Thanks to his five months of forced convalescence his penis had fully recovered from the attentions of BloJob – of which he of course knew nothing - and he was keen to get back in the saddle again, as it were.

Unfortunately for Blond his doctors had confined him to his room whilst they carried out a series of tests aimed at trying to find out why he had lost part of his memory; and the two nurses who cared for him round the clock, although excellent nurses, were not his type of female companion at all, one of them being plain and the other one fat. However after the first week had passed painfully slowly there was a definite upturn on the attractive girl front in the shape of a temporary recruit to the nursing staff. And what a shape! The nurse, who was covering for the illness of the fat nurse, had a figure to die for. And James Blond was soon dying for it.

Blond judged the girl to be around five feet eight inches tall. The ideal height for a woman in Blond's opinion; shorter than his six feet two, so that she would have to stretch up on tiptoes to be kissed, but not so much shorter that he had but to merely bend his neck slightly so that their lips might meet. Which they would be doing in the not too distant future if it were anything to do with Blond.

The nurse's uniform, an outfit consisting of a starched blue gingham dress, spotless white pinafore and hat, and black stockings, was designed to be functional rather than flattering, but there is only so much that a nurse's uniform can do to hide a woman's physical charms and in the case of the vision now smiling at Blond it was fighting a losing battle.

"Good evening, Mr Blond," she smiled. "What would you like for supper this evening?"

"You," said Blond, hungrily, with a rakish smile.

She admonished him with a wagging finger, but in a light-hearted way, her smile still radiant. "Cheeky."

The girl was as beautiful as she was shapely, reminding Blond of the young Brigitte Bardot; the same full lips and Bambi eyes, the same pert nose that wrinkled coquettishly when she smiled. It was a face that excited Blond. And nothing excited Blond more than a beautiful woman. He patted the bed beside him. "Come, sit down and tell me all about yourself, Nurse....?"

"Shag. Ava Shag."

Blond smiled. "Thanks very much, get your knickers down."

"If I'd had a shag for every time I'd heard that I'd have had a lot of shags," smiled the nurse.

At this Blond's heart started to beat faster. Then it went into overdrive as Nurse Shag sat down on the bed beside him, close enough for him to touch her.

He caught the scent of her perfume. It had the effect of exciting him even more. He put his hands on her shoulders and pulled her gently towards him. She came entirely willingly, melting into his arms. They kissed. Immediately their lips met the tip of her tongue penetrated his mouth. Blond reciprocated. It was a long kiss, a kiss that was all that could be expected of a kiss, all that Blond had hoped it might be. But now he wanted more than a kiss. He wanted what a kiss could lead to. Unwillingly he disengaged his lips from hers, looked deeply into her eyes and said: "Say you'll make love with me, Ava."

"Well I would," said the nurse. "But I can't."

Blond was puzzled. "Can't? What do you mean, you can't?"

"I'm having my period."

Blond could scarcely believe his ears. "Having your period?"

"Yes. Sorry."

"But....I mean you can't be....the girls I meet are never having their period."

"Well I'm having mine," said the nurse, simply.

Blond still couldn't accept the situation. He persisted. "But....I mean you just can't be. That never happens to me."

Nurse Shag got up off the bed, now starting to get a little annoyed with this man who wouldn't take no for an answer. "Look, just tell me what you want for your supper would you."

But Blond didn't want any supper. His appetite had disappeared along with the realization that for the very first time in his career as a secret agent he wasn't going to get his way with a woman, and for a reason he had never come up against before.

Blond never saw Ava Shag again. The following night the fat nurse was back on duty so he was never to know what might have happened had the lovely nurse put in another appearance. Would he have propositioned her again if she had? Periods didn't last forever and Nurse Shag's might have been over by then, but her turning him down had given his ego a severe jolt. Apart from that it would have been embarrassing if he'd propositioned her again and she was still in the same situation she'd been the night before. And anyway, he consoled himself, there would be other girls, just as there always had been, so why take the risk of embarrassing himself?

*

Dr Snodgrass, the consultant assigned to Blond's case, had become very concerned about Blond's bladder problem.

When Blond had come out of his coma he had been confined to bed and when he needed to pass water he had only to ask the nurse for a bottle. However after ten days had passed and with Blond getting stronger by the day Dr Snodgrass had allowed him out of bed, and now when duty called, which it did with all its old frequency, Blond had to walk down the passage to the gents' toilet some fifty yards away. The plain nurse had brought this to Dr Snodgrass's attention, one thing had led to another, and Blond, against his better judgement, had allowed Dr Snodgrass to talk him into letting one of the hospital's specialists, Dr Dongh, give him an examination with a view to alleviating the problem. An appointment had been arranged for the following day and the examination duly carried out, or at least it had been carried out until Blond's head had crashed into Dr Dongh's surgery wall and his memory had magically returned.

CHAPTER NINETEEN

INTO THE CAVERN

On arriving back in Stockport Blond immediately made for the Façade factory. If Goldnojaws were still in residence Blond would assassinate him and the matter would be over and done with. Since he would be using his license to kill there would be no repercussions. There never were when the security of the country was at stake. However when Blond pulled up outside Façade and observed immediately that the windows which had previously been blacked out were now transparent he feared that Goldnojaws had flown the coop.

He got out of the car and pressed his nose to one of the windows. Sadly his suspicions were confirmed; the room had been cleared of all Professor Gonzalez's laboratory equipment and glass tanks and was now completely empty. A minute later he was stepping into the reception area of Façade. Goldnojaws' secretary was typing at her desk. Blond marched up to her. Wasting no time on formalities he said: "Is your boss here?"

The secretary looked up from her keyboard. She recognised Blond immediately. Her nostrils flared. "You! The male chauvinistic pig who drugged my Turkish Delight."

Blond contained his temper. "I enquired of you if Goldnojaws was here?"

"You almost lost me my job!"

Blond regarded her testily. "Are you sure the reason you almost lost your job isn't because you are going deaf? Because I've already asked you twice if Goldnojaws is here and you appear not to have heard me."

The secretary sneered at him. "Take a hike."

She made to return to her keyboard but before you could say QWERTY Blond had taken a step forward, balled his hand into a fist and hit her once, very hard, on the point of the jaw. It would be some time before she typed or got ratty with anyone again.

He stepped over her, made for Goldnojaws' office and flung the door open. He noticed at once that the photographs of the crane fly and the locust had gone from the walls, as had the large map of Stockport. The occupant of the office, a fat red-faced man with ginger hair, half rose from his desk, startled. "What the...!"

"Nothing to be alarmed about," Blond assured him. He quickly established his credentials and on questioning the new occupant of the office learned that he was the factory's new owner. Goldnojaws had sold him the business lock, stock and barrel some two months previously for a knock down price, and no, he didn't have any idea where the dwarf could be found. Blond thanked him and left.

As he slipped back behind the wheel of his car Blond speculated as to where Goldnojaws might be. Anywhere in Stockport, he supposed. Or anywhere else for that matter. However he was almost certain that the dwarf would have set up his new HQ within the town's limits, it would appeal to his warped sense of humour to be living amongst the people who had forced him out of his place of birth and upon whom he would very soon be exacting a terrible revenge.

But where in Stockport? One of the places he had bought? Casino Royale perhaps? The football ground? The Pyramid building? For no other reason than he had to start somewhere Blond headed for the Pyramid building. On the way there he had to pee, his prostate condition now worse if anything, probably thanks to Dr Dongh's probing index finger. Fortunately the only public toilets in Stockport so far as Blond knew, situated in the Merseyway Shopping Precinct, were more or less on the way to the Pyramid building and not too far distant.

In fact the entrance to the toilets was almost exactly opposite the Air Raid Shelters and when Blond emerged from the gents after relieving himself he was surprised to observe that not only had the reception area at the Air Raid Shelters not been demolished and replaced by Goldnojaws' promised ten storey department store but that the Air Raid Shelter complex itself was still open for business. It was by no means the only surprise the secret agent would receive that day.

Intrigued, Blond crossed the road and entered the Air Raid Shelters complex. The same sprightly old guide he had spoken to on his previous visit almost six months earlier was still employed there, now even sprightlier than before if anything. "Oh yes, we're still here," he beamed, when Blond expressed his surprise that the place was still open. "Yes, Dr Goldnojaws, bless him – he's the new owner – he had a change of heart."

This news didn't surprise Blond. If Goldnojaws was capable of buying a football ground, a casino and four bowling greens the adding of the Air Raid Shelters to his list of red herrings would be par for the course. But what then of the dwarf's plan to excavate ten thousand square metres of earth from below the shelter? "So the place didn't close down after all then?" he asked.

The old guide chuckled. "Oh it closed all right. Yes, we've only been re-opened a couple of weeks." He puffed out his chest a little. "With all the staff on twenty per cent more money. And back pay from when we was sacked, thanks to the generosity of Dr Goldnojaws."

Thanks to Dr Goldnojaws wanting to make sure you and the rest of the staff don't get too nosey about what he's doing here, thought Blond.

The guide went on. "Yes, the word is that Dr Goldnojaws is going into the wine importing business in a big way." He leaned forward slightly to take Blond into his confidence. "We are now standing over what will one day be the world's biggest wine cellar."

Blond looked suitably impressed. "Really?"

"They were dynamiting and digging and bringing out rocks for near on three months. I swear they'd have dug through clear to Australia if they'd taken any more out."

So that was how Goldnojaws had managed to remove ten thousand square metres of sandstone from beneath the streets of Stockport without anyone concerning themselves too much about it - he'd told them he was creating wine cellars. If only they knew what was probably down there right now. Not claret and burgundy but instant death! Not Cotes du Rhone and Hermitage and Cote Rotie and Cornas but ten feet long superlocusts!

Something began to nag at Blond. How had the workmen managed to get out such a vast quantity of sandstone without disturbing the Air Raid Shelters reception area?

"Oh they disturbed it all right," said the old guide, when Blond asked him. "Dismantled every last bit of it, brick by brick. Then when they'd finished the wine cellar they put it all back together again, just like it was Lego." The guide looked around him, proudly. "To look at it you'd never know the old place had been touched, would you."

"Indeed." Blond was anxious to get a look at the 'wine cellar'. He quizzed the old man. "This wine cellar? It can be accessed from the air raid shelters I take it?"

The guide shook his head. "Funny thing that, but no. Well as far as I know it can't. There's just a brick wall right at the end of the lowest level; I suppose it's behind that, but there's no door or anything. The entrance must be somewhere else."

Yes and I know where it is, thought Blond, recalling his time at the mercy of Goldnojaws when the dwarf had outlined his plan. The Pyramid building.

*

The day Blond's memory had returned all the events of the previous four weeks had come flooding back, Dr Goldnojaws and his diabolical plan to let loose a plague of superlocusts on the town of Stockport at the very forefront. One of the first things the secret agent had recollected was that Goldnojaws had said that his terrible scheme would be launched in six months time. Blond had realised with horror that by this time that fateful day was just one week away.

He had had to get to Stockport right away, there wasn't a second to lose. He was fully aware that he should first report all he knew to Maddox, but he was equally aware that if he did his boss would probably take him off the case due to his long period of hospitalization. Maddox could be very protective of his staff, especially his secret agents, and Blond envisaged his boss insisting that he remain in hospital until he was fully recovered. Which was the last thing he wanted.

The first thing he wanted was a sight of Goldnojaws. So he could kill him. Blond knew that if he were to eliminate Goldnojaws the dwarf's monstrous plan would die with him. Gonzalez would have no interest in seeing it through, even if he'd had the desire; the bio chemist was a follower not a leader. Besides, his interest had been in the breeding of the superlocusts, his job would now be over and in all probability Goldnojaws would have paid him off and he would be off the scene altogether. And there were no other interested parties so far as Blond knew; Dr Goldnojaws was a loner, his show a one-man band, a horrific one man ego-charged comeback appearance.

Blond did however call in at HQ before leaving London and heading for Stockport. In his desk he had a key to the underground garage beneath Paramount Properties. In the garage was Blond's Lagonda, six and a half litres of supercharged pure macho fitted out with the very latest in high tech crime fighting devices. No one saw Blond enter the garage. No one saw him leave five minutes later driving the treasured Lagonda.

*

On arriving at the Pyramid building Blond noticed that several alterations had been made since he'd last seen it. Now all the panes of glass were the same dark blue, whereas before about ten per cent of them had been plain glass, along with a few amber coloured ones. The blue glass was of the type that you can see out of but can't see through, so with the elimination of the plain and amber glass it was impossible to see what was going on inside the Pyramid – a necessary precaution considering what Goldnojaws intended to inhabit the place with, reflected Blond.

The other alterations were constructional. Previously the Pyramid had ended in a point. Now the top of it was flat, the top fifteen or so feet of it having been lopped off. Blond suspected that the top of the structure would now probably incorporate a sliding roof - there would have to be some way for the superlocusts to get out when Goldnojaws decided to unleash them on the unsuspecting Stockport public. The final alteration was to the large entrance doors to the Pyramid, which had been replaced by much smaller wooden double doors, the only part of the building apart from the metal framework that wasn't glass.

Blond noted that there was also a small single-storey office block, not much bigger than a bungalow, that hadn't been there before, close by the Pyramid.

There appeared to be no security whatsoever. At first Blond was surprised at this omission, given Goldnojaws' plans, before he concluded that barbed wire fences and guard patrols would only draw attention to the building, whereas without these security measures the Pyramid stated that it had nothing worth securing and in consequence might be left alone. Well James Blond for one wasn't going to leave it alone!

On trying the new door to the Pyramid Blond found it was locked, as he knew it would be. He then tried the door to the office block. That too was locked. He peered in through the windows. Just normal offices, two. Plus a sort of sitting room furnished with an antique leather Chesterfield and a couple of matching chairs and a coffee table. No one was in any of the rooms. If this was Goldnojaws' new HQ he was elsewhere at the moment. Well maybe Goldnojaws wasn't around but the cavern he'd created under the Air Raid Shelters for his monstrous superlocusts certainly was. It would be Blond's next port of call.

He collected his torch from the Lagonda and returned to the Pyramid. His skeleton key had the door open in seconds. He quickly stepped inside. The building was quite empty. He saw the entrance to the tunnel about twenty yards away and made his way over to it. As promised by Goldnojaws the tunnel, hewed from the soft red sandstone, was about five metres wide. He shone the torch into its depths. It illuminated the black void for maybe fifty yards. He set off on the journey down, keeping the beam of the torch directed at the ground a couple or so yards in front of him. He didn't want to risk tripping over any loose stones or debris that might have been left lying around which might cause him to drop his torch and maybe break it.

The gradient was minimal, no more than about 1 in 50 Blond estimated. His destination below the Air Raid Shelters was more or less two miles away. It was comfortable walking, the floor relatively smooth, whatever stray stones there were being small and few and far between, and he made good progress. Every so often he stopped and shone the torch down the tunnel. The view was always the same, a smooth narrowing cylinder hewn out of the rock, disappearing into the gloom.

He had been walking for about a mile when the torch picked out something other than the sandstone walls and small rocks, and no more than fifty yards away. Blond froze. It was one of the superlocusts. And it was heading his way. He snapped off the torch, pressed his back to the wall of the tunnel and waited, hardly daring to draw breath. Twenty seconds later he sensed as much as saw and heard the giant creature lumbering slowly past him. He gave it another twenty seconds then directed the beam of the torch back up the tunnel. The mutant was thirty yards past him and heading for the Pyramid. The nightmare had begun.

The scene that greeted Blond when he reached the vast underground cavern some fifteen minutes later was like something dreamed up by H G Wells' more imaginative brother on acid. Superlocusts covered the entire floor space, three, four, even five deep in places. The stench, from the discarded rotting chrysalises, was horrendous. Only a very few of the mutants were fully developed, maybe one in twenty Blond guessed, but some of them weren't far from maturity and the rest of them not too far behind. At the rate insects developed he knew it would be only a matter of days rather than weeks before they were fully grown.

Blond was on the fringe of the vast pile of giant insects. Beyond them, maybe a hundred and fifty yards away, he could just make out a single-storey red brick building, about thirty feet long. The fluorescent lights shining through its windows lit up its immediate surroundings, the only light in the cavern apart from his torch. Was it where Goldnojaws was holed up? Blond would have loved to know but there was no way of finding out, no passage through the seething, stinking mass of bodies, and even if there had been there was no way of knowing how the superlocusts would react if he were to venture among them.

And he was no use to anybody dead. Not that he feared death - as a Secret Service agent he expected to die before his time, premature death being an occupational hazard, a likelihood if not a downright certainty - but he had no intention of dying before he had disposed of Goldnojaws.

He did an about face and started back up the tunnel. After the superlocust had passed him on his way down a further three of the huge insects had gone by him on their way to the Pyramid. Even in the short time he'd been in the cavern another one had disengaged itself from the others and had started to make its way up the tunnel. It was time for action. And fast.

CHAPTER TWENTY

DAMNED

"Blond! Dash it all man, where the hell have you been?"

Blond closed Maddox's office door behind him and turned to face the wrath of his boss. "Sorry sir, allow me to explain."

"I think you better had, and fast. And it had better be damn good. Good God man we've had every policeman in the country on the lookout for you, not to mention half the Secret Service!"

Blond quickly gave Maddox chapter and verse, holding nothing back, from the time he'd gone to Stockport initially up until his second visit twenty four hours earlier, and what had happened subsequently. When he had finished Maddox's anger had completely disappeared, to be replaced by grave concern.

"There isn't a second to waste, sir," Blond urged, "If we are to save Stockport."

Maddox slowly nodded his head. "Yes. And with it the world from what you say." He balled his hand and brought it crashing down on the desk. "Damn Goldnojaws!" Having expended his anger he took out his pipe and tobacco pouch, needing the solace of a smoke (although by no means a quantum of it). "Any ideas as to how we can put paid to this fiend, James?"

"A couple, sir."

"Good man. Fire away."

Since emerging from the Pyramid Blond had thought of little else other than ways of preventing the wholesale carnage that Goldnojaws intended to bring down on Stockport.

For some reason Blond always thought more clearly, with much greater concentration, when he was driving. It was the reason he'd chosen to report to Maddox in person rather than over the phone - the hundred and eighty mile journey would afford him three or four hours of undisturbed thought. It had been whilst he was driving that he'd come up with the idea that had finally killed the world domination aspirations of the Italian olive oil magnate Count Bartelloni. As his deep concentration tended to discount his driving skills somewhat it had also killed the four Frenchmen who were dining al fresco outside a Montpellier café, when he had failed to see a red light at a crossroads and caused a Citroen CV8 to plough into them. However if Blond had been pushed about the accident he would have replied that the loss of the lives of four Frenchmen was a small price to pay if it were instrumental in stopping the world from being dominated by an Eyetie.

Likewise the drive south from Stockport had not been without incident, as the driver of a Ford Fiesta in Highbury could testify, after Blond had failed to stop at a give way sign and caused the Fiesta driver to crash into a lamppost and sustain a broken leg. If asked to comment on the incident Blond would have said that although the cost was much greater compared to the incident in the Count Bartelloni case, a British broken leg as opposed to four French lives, the price was still fully justified.

Blond got down to brass tacks with Maddox. "First we'll need the assistance of the RAF, sir."

Maddox looked dubious and shook his head. "Oh I'm not sure about that, James. You know how I feel about involving the military unless it's absolutely necessary. Especially the Brylcreem Boys. It will be some time before I forget the Madagascar affair when they accidentally blew up that fertilizer factory."

Blond now saw an opportunity to convince Maddox. He stroked his jaw thoughtfully. "Yes, that caused a hell of a *stink* I believe, sir."

Despite the grave situation Maddox's face lit up. "Oh excellent one-liner, James, excellent. You're really getting into it now."

"Yes I've realised you were right all along, sir," said Blond. He paused and looked keenly at Maddox. "As I am equally sure you'll realise that the involvement of the RAF is absolutely vital to my plan."

"You'd better explain then."

Blond smiled to himself. Humour could be useful in his job after all. He took a deep breath. "Well I'm fairly certain the floor of the cavern that houses the superlocusts is well below the level of the River Mersey, which itself is hard by the cavern, if not directly over it. Dropping a powerful bomb, or bombs, would breach the river bed and the Mersey would flood the cavern. And unless our friend Goldnojaws has taught his superlocusts to do the breast stroke that would be the end of them."

Maddox looked thoughtful. "Well there's little doubt the RAF could do it; dash it all, nowadays with smart bombs and the like they could probably successfully hit a dustbin lid from fifty thousand feet. But it would take a hell of a lot of organising. We can't just start dropping bombs in the centre of Stockport. Even if you wouldn't notice a great deal of difference after we've done it, from what I remember of the place. I mean there's the possible loss of life to consider."

"There is the definite loss of life to consider if we don't, sir. I'm afraid it's a case of damned if we do and damned if we don't."

Maddox chewed on the problem for a moment. "We could completely clear the area I suppose. Say a half mile radius. The military would know more precisely how much. It would be a pig to organise but I don't see any alternative."

"How long, sir? To organise it?"

Maddox spread his hands. "Twenty four hours, forty eight."

"I wouldn't like to delay it an hour longer than forty eight."

"No." Maddox rubbed his chin thoughtfully. He came to a decision. "Right, that's the way forward then." He looked questioningly at Blond. "But you said you had a couple of ideas, James? What's the other one?"

"To my certain knowledge there are four of the superlocusts in the Pyramids building already. It's a near certainty more of them will have already made the trip up from the cavern while I was making the trip to London. Lord knows how many of them will be there in two days time. Fifty? A hundred? Your guess is as good as mine. They will all have to be eliminated."

Maddox took this on board, chewed on it for a moment, then said: "I'm thinking this might be a job for the SAS, James. Storm the place, shoot them dead."

"With respect sir, you haven't seen the superlocusts. They're as good as armour-plated. It's going to take more than a bullet to knock them out. Even an explosive bullet. We're talking rocket launchers here."

"Then so be it, if that's what it's going to take."

"Not so fast, sir. You're forgetting that the Pyramid is made of glass. A stray shell, the glass shatters, in the bat of an eyelid we could have a hundred superlocusts swarming over Stockport hunting for likely prey."

Maddox shook his head. "Hmm, hadn't thought of that." He was silent for a moment, his mind working overtime. He looked at Blond keenly. "Tear gas?"

"The first thing I thought of; but the superlocusts would probably take refuge in the tunnel."

"So what to do? Is there an alternative to the SAS?"

Blond nodded and told Maddox what was in his mind. When he'd finished speaking his boss looked at him gravely and said: "You would be putting yourself at great risk James. You do realise that?" Blond nodded. "But if you think you can pull it off...?"

"There's only one way to find out, sir."

CHAPTER TWENTY ONE

BACK INTO THE CAVERN

The air strike by three RAF Jaguar attack/reconnaissance aircraft, each armed with a Pathway III 2000 pound bomb, took place at 9 a.m. two days after Blond's meeting in London with Maddox. It was entirely successful insofar as when the River Mersey was breached whatever superlocusts were in the cavern below were immediately engulfed in the torrent, and perished by drowning. However, at the precise moment the bombs struck the superlocusts weren't the only occupants of the cavern. James Blond was down there too.

*

Blond had travelled back to Stockport in the early hours of the morning of the scheduled air strike. Over the previous two days Maddox and his staff had moved heaven and earth in order to organise everything in time.

It had been decided at Cabinet level that the entire area to a radius of one mile from the target would be made an exclusion zone and be cleared of every living thing. The whole operation was kept as covert as was humanly possible, there being a real fear that if Goldnojaws got wind of the plan he might precipitate his attack on Stockport earlier than planned, with the consequent loss of countless lives and the probable decimation of much of the town.

From 4 a.m. that morning all traffic attempting to enter Stockport town centre was re-routed around the town. All police leave had been cancelled and the entire Stockport police force, save for those responsible for stopping the traffic and those throwing sickies, augmented by two hundred officers from adjoining forces, formed a perimeter round the town to ensure that anyone travelling on foot didn't enter its limits.

Most of the people normally found in Stockport at 9 a.m. are office workers and shop assistants. The previous evening, just before leaving work for the day, they were all informed that they had been given the following day off on full pay, no questions asked. The Government would foot the bill.

Few people lived within the designated danger area, no more than a couple of thousand, the majority of them housed in flats, the remainder in houses. The occupants, along with their pets, had been moved to places of safety late the previous evening. No one was forgotten. Against the Chief Constable's private wishes, the top policeman seeing it as an ideal opportunity to get rid of a few of the town's undesirables, the police force had scoured all the favourite places frequented by the local down-and-outs. Any old lags, druggies and dossers rooted out had been given a free meal and accommodation for the night, accompanied by a stern warning not to return. All, so far as could be determined, had been located, all had complied.

Blond now drew up outside the Pyramid building. He checked his watch. 8.30 a.m. He had exactly half an hour to carry out his daring plan.

There were no lights on in the nearby office. It was now daylight so Blond had one last look through the windows to see if Goldnojaws was in residence. He wasn't. If he had been Blond would have assassinated him there and then and called off the air strike.

However it was not to be as simple as that, so things would have to be done the hard way, and in an hour's time an estimated one hundred thousand square metres of the centre of Stockport would disappear from the face of the earth. It was Blond's fervent hope that Goldnojaws was down the cavern and that he would disappear along with it.

Blond drove the Lagonda up to the door of the Pyramid, got out and opened the boot. It was brimful of fruit and vegetables, most of it well past its sell by date, and the stench that greeted him caused him to recoil in disgust.

Blond firmly believed in the maxim of 'tried and tested', so never wasted time looking for a new idea when an old one would suffice. In this instance the old idea was the one he'd employed when dealing with the giant rats in the Dr Zog case. If it had been successful in luring the giant rats towards the White Cliffs of Dover and ultimately to their death, why shouldn't it work to lure the superlocusts back down the tunnel to the cavern? They would be ravenously hungry, Blond suspected. Well he had some food for them!

Blond had asked the greengrocer to include plenty overripe examples in the consignment of fruit and vegetables he'd ordered as he wanted to make absolutely sure that the superlocusts picked up the scent. It might have been a case of one bad apple, but Blond suspected that the greengrocer had seized upon his request as an opportunity to offload whatever rotting stock he had on his hands that day. Blond, his eyes beginning to water, pinched his nostrils together and grimaced, for the smell was truly awful. However he consoled himself that the superlocusts certainly wouldn't experience any difficulty in picking up the scent and following his trail.

Satisfied, Blond let himself into the Pyramid building, swung the doors open wide and drove the Lagonda through. He visibly gasped as he took in the sight before him. There must have been two hundred or more of the superlocusts now in residence inside the Pyramid. Most of them were on the floor, the rest were clinging to the walls. Uncannily, they were all quite still, almost as though waiting for the signal to move.

Blond quickly closed the doors behind him – the last thing he wanted was some of the superlocusts escaping; even if so much as a single one of the hideous looking mutants escaped it would be enough to cause terror on the streets.

Back behind the wheel Blond drove slowly to the entrance of the tunnel. A couple of the superlocusts were in his path and as the car approached them they ambled aside with a singular lack of interest. He pulled up at the entrance to the tunnel, the Lagonda's nose pointing down into the depths, and prayed that the superlocusts would follow him.

He checked through the rear view mirror. None of the superlocusts had moved. He reversed back to within a couple of feet of the nearest of them. It showed not the slightest interest. Blond's heart sank. What had worked with the giant rats clearly wasn't going to work with the superlocusts.

He switched on his mobile phone. Maddox would have to be informed and the contingency plan set in motion. The Pyramid would be sealed off and the following day another air strike would be made, this time on the Pyramid building, with the consequent devastation to the surrounding area. As this included a large section of the M60 motorway the cost would be counted in hundreds of millions of pounds.

Blond had just got through to Maddox and had started to report the situation when he sensed a movement behind him. He turned to look through the rear window. One of the superlocusts was on the point of swallowing a large melon, plucked from the boot of the Lagonda by its great mouth. Two other superlocusts were showing an interest. Blond punched the air in delight. They were taking the bait! They were falling for it! Another three superlocusts now joined the others. Blond quickly informed Maddox that he was back in business, gently pressed his foot on the accelerator and slowly started the two mile journey down the tunnel. He checked in the rear view mirror. The superlocusts were following, like so many sheep, like so many rats following the Pied Piper once again.

Blond settled into the journey, driving just fast enough to keep clear of the superlocusts, not wanting the nearest of them to gobble up all the bait before he'd lured them all the way back down to the cavern, where they would either perish in the blast of the bombs or drown in the aftermath of the explosion. Five miles an hour turned out to be the right speed, fast enough to keep them at bay, slow enough to keep them interested. Twenty five minutes later Blond entered the cavern. By now it was absolutely seething with the superlocusts, only a very few of them not yet fully grown.

It was not a sight on which to linger for too long and having delivered all the superlocusts to the cavern Blond's inclination was to turn the Lagonda round and head back up the tunnel without delay. However circumstances didn't allow this.

When he had brought the Lagonda to a halt the superlocusts immediately behind him had fallen on the contents of the boot and devoured them in seconds. However Blond reasoned that the boot would still probably carry the scent of the fruit and vegetables, maybe a strong enough scent to draw the attention of the superlocusts, who then might follow him back up the tunnel.

He looked at his watch. 8.50. Ten minutes to go until the first bomb was due to strike. He decided to give it another five minutes to give the scent the chance to dissipate, then to commence the journey back up the tunnel.

Suddenly he noticed lights in the low building he'd seen on his previous visit. He wondered if Goldnojaws was in there. He hoped so. It would be nothing less than justice if the dwarf were to perish at the same time and in the same manner as his abominable creations.

Having thought of the possibility Blond now felt compelled to find out for definite. Hoping Goldnojaws would perish wasn't enough. He had to know. He started up the Lagonda and began to nose it slowly through the superlocusts. As he drew nearer to the building he switched off the headlights and used the light from the building's windows to guide him.

Two minutes later he was outside the door. He eased himself out of the Lagonda, and keeping a wary eye on the superlocusts went quickly to one of the windows. He looked in. His jaw dropped in amazement. Goldnojaws was there all right. And the wretched Professor Gonzalez too. But so was BloJob! How could that be? It couldn't, he had killed her. He had seen her head depart from her body. He screwed his eyes tight shut, shook his head, then looked at her again. No. He was wrong. It wasn't BloJob. This woman wasn't quite as tall as BloJob had been, but was even heftier, and her hair colouring was different, more an auburn colour than yellow. A sister, maybe? BloJob's sister? Well whoever she was she would soon be getting a rude awakening.

Satisfied that Goldnojaws would die along with Gonzalez, Blond was about to get back into the Lagonda and return to the Pyramid when suddenly two huge, powerful arms encircled him and lifted him clean off his feet. Struggling, kicking, he twisted his head round in an effort to get a view of his assailant. With a gasp he saw that it was someone who looked very much like BloJob who had grabbed him, and was now muscling him towards the door! Another BloJob? Another sister? Three BloJob sisters? Christ Almighty, as if the Beverly Sisters hadn't been bad enough!

The second BloJob sister kicked open the door and threw Blond unceremoniously into the room. He staggered on the wooden floor before falling in a heap at the feet of Goldnojaws. The dwarf almost jumped out of his skin at the sudden intrusion. Then his face lit up as he recognised the figure on the floor. "Blond!"

Blond got to his knees and scowled at his adversary. "Yes, Blond, Goldnojaws."

"You live!"

"Indeed."

Both BloJob sisters hovered menacingly over Blond. One of them pointed a gnarled finger at him and looked at Goldnojaws. "This the bastard who killed my little sister?"

The sister who had grabbed Blond, the same height as her sister but even heftier said: "Is this the motherfucking cocksucking arsehole, Goldie?"

"Yes, that is James Blond," said Goldnojaws. He allowed his lip to curl in a smirk before adding: "Very soon to be the late James Blond." He stabbed a finger at Blond. "Kill him!"

"Too fucking right," snarled the heftier BloJob sister. She grabbed hold of Blond, wrenched him to his feet as though he were a rag doll and raised him high overhead as if to hurl him to the ground.

"Wait!" cried Blond, in desperation. "Before I die. Don't you want to know how I killed BloJob, Goldnojaws?"

It was a shot in the dark. Blond had managed a glance at his watch. It had told him that the time was three minutes to nine, just three short minutes away from the time the first of the bombs was due to strike. His ploy just might buy him those three minutes and the chance to escape.

Goldnojaws held up a hand, just in time to stop the sister hurling Blond to the concrete floor, and bellowed: "Stop! Put him down. But hold him securely. Both of you."

The other sister joined them and each sister now clamped Blond's arms in an iron grip.

Goldnojaws regarded Blond. "Well, Mr Blond?"

"I told her a joke."

"What?"

"I told BloJob a joke. And she died laughing. Literally laughed her head off."

Goldnojaws was incredulous. "You killed BloJob with a joke?"

From the depths of his mind Blond had recalled that along with the hundred one-liners supplied by the Blind Date scriptwriter ten all purpose jokes had been included. The third of them would suit the present scenario perfectly, with a little personalising. Maybe there was something in this business of having humour in one's armoury after all?

"Yes," said Blond. "I told her that one day a friend of Dr Goldnojaws fixed him up with a blind date. When Goldnojaws turned up he found that the girl, although very beautiful, was about six feet tall. They decided to go for a walk, and despite their difference in height they hit it off immediately. After they had been walking for about four miles the girl squeezed Goldnojaws' hand and said 'I like you. I like you a lot'.

And Goldnojaws said: 'And I like you a lot'.

'You're cute,' said the girl. 'Would you like to make love to me?'

Goldnojaws said: 'Try and stop me'.

The girl said: 'But there's a bit of a problem. I only like to make love standing up'.

'No problem,' said Goldnojaws, 'I'll stand on something.'

He looked around for something to stand on and spotted a discarded blacksmith's anvil. 'That will do fine,' he said.

So he stood on the anvil and they made love. When they'd finished the girl said: 'That was lovely, really lovely'.

Goldnojaws said: 'It's not the size of the cannon it's the force of the cannonball'.

'We can do it again later if you like', said the girl.

'I like', said Goldnojaws.

So they set off back the way they had come. After they'd been walking about a mile Goldnojaws said: 'Are you ready to make love again?'

'Not just yet,' the girl said. 'I'm still glowing from the first time. You were really fantastic'.

After they'd walked another mile Goldnojaws said: 'Are you ready to make love now?'

'Almost. Just give it a little bit longer,' the girl said.

They walked another mile. Goldnojaws said: 'Well now are you ready to make love again?'

'Do you know something?' the girl said. 'I've gone right off the idea of doing it again'.

Goldnojaws looked at her and said: 'Do you mean to tell me I've been carrying this fucking anvil all this way and….'

"And BloJob laughed her head off," said Blond.

Goldnojaws was absolutely livid. Red in the face, veins standing out, quivering with hate he raged: "And now you too will die Mr Blond! But it won't be through laughing, it will…."

At that moment the first of the 2000 pound bombs exploded overhead. The building literally shook and every window shattered into a thousand pieces. Seizing his opportunity Blond shook himself free of the startled BloJob sisters and leapt out of one of the windows. Rolling over he picked himself up and jumped into the Lagonda a split second before the second bomb struck. The second strike breached the river and in an instant a million gallons of the River Mersey came flooding into the cavern. With a loud crack the building housing Goldnojaws and his cohorts broke in half and the roof fell in on them.

Within seconds the water level was up to the bonnet of the Lagonda. Ten seconds later it was entirely covered. Blond switched on the headlights and selected main beam. In front of him was a sea of drowning superlocusts. He waited for a full minute, by which time the cavern was completely filled with water and most of the superlocusts had perished. The rest would soon be following them into oblivion.

Blond switched the Lagonda to submarine mode and set off back up the tunnel to the Pyramid and safety.

CHAPTER TWENTY TWO

A CHANGE OF HEART

It was a month after the successful conclusion of the Goldnojaws affair that the next episode in the attempt to get to the bottom of Blond's prostate troubles took place. His situation hadn't got any worse, but then it hadn't got any better, and wasn't going to get any better without treatment. As Blond had finally been forced to admit, it was something that needed to be addressed, sorted out once and for all.

The letter from the hospital had called it a bladder examination. Nothing to worry about there then. A bit dodgy-sounding, but nothing to a man who had already endured a bowel examination, a procedure that involved having a finger rammed up his anus, and some years earlier had had a stomach examination, a procedure which involved a camera being forcibly shoved down his throat. It would be difficult to say which of those two previous invasions of his body had caused Blond the most distress, the pain and embarrassment of the former being about equal in intensity to the pain and discomfort of the latter. What is certain is that even if they had both been carried out at the same time the experience wouldn't have been one tenth as harrowing a procedure as the bladder examination turned out to be.

Blond hadn't really thought much about how the nurse was actually going to examine his bladder but if he had been asked to hazard a guess he would have suggested that it might be something not dissimilar to having an X-ray of the digestive system following the taking of a barium meal. He couldn't have been more wrong.

As requested Blond had undressed and put on the smock-like garment beloved of hospitals, the item of clothing for which you need the abilities of a contortionist to successfully tie the strings at the back, and which, if by some miracle you have managed to tie them, need the skills of Houdini to untie them, and was now seated nonchalantly with his legs dangling over the side of the operating table awaiting the ministrations of the nurse who was to carry out the procedure. He hadn't observed anything overtly pain-inflicting amongst the apparatus laid out in antiseptic neatness on the nearby table, so it was more to make conversation than a search for knowledge that he asked the nurse what the two long thin plastic tubes were for.

"The catheters? I insert them in your penis and push them down into your bladder," she said, matter of fact.

"Down my penis?" Blond asked, with disbelief.

The nurse nodded.

Blond gulped. "Both the tubes?"

The nurse affirmed this with another curt nod.

"At the same time?"

The nurse nodded a third time. Blond didn't press her for any more details as he was sure it would only elicit another nod and he wasn't at all sure he would be able to handle all the things she'd already nodded for, never mind another.

"There'll be a bit of discomfort," the nurse said.

This snippet of information seemed to Blond to be about as necessary as telling someone who was about to be hung, drawn and quartered that it wasn't going to be a picnic. Then it occurred to him that being hung, drawn and quartered might be preferable to the bladder examination and he was just about to ask the nurse if this was an option, and if it was could he take it, when she went into action.

"Lie down please, Mr Blond," she said, snapping on a pair of rubber gloves in the expert, businesslike way that medical staff do, probably in the hope that it demonstrates their efficiency, when all it does is help to fill one with an even greater sense of dread.

The only saving grace so far as Blond could see was that the nurse was fat. A possible conquest she wasn't. So at least he would be spared the embarrassment of a spontaneous erection when she handled his penis.

"This will help deaden the pain," the nurse said, spraying his genital area with an aerosol. Having done this, and waited ten seconds or so for the anaesthetic to take effect, she picked up one of the catheters and eyed Blond ominously.

Blond clamped his eyes firmly shut. He had no wish to see what the nurse was about to do with the catheter, feeling it would be quite bad enough.

The nurse went about her business. It was immediately obvious to Blond that at the moment he closed his eyes she had swapped the catheter for a length of Dyno-Rod for surely it was something capable of clearing blocked drains that she was now shoving down his penis with gay abandon.

Blond had no way of knowing whether the anaesthetic spray had helped to deaden the pain, but felt that if it had it was wasting its time, for the pain was truly excruciating. When he had been in the Royal Marines prior to joining the Secret Service one of his compatriots had been unfortunate enough to catch gonorrhoea, the symptoms of which, the man had said, were 'Like pissing broken glass'. By the time the two catheters had been pushed into his penis as far as the nurse deemed sufficient Blond felt like he was pissing not broken glass but broken bottles, and bottles of magnum and jeroboam proportions at that.

The catheters inserted, Blond was then bidden by the nurse to stand up and gather his smock round his waist so that it didn't foul the plastic pipes now dangling from his penis, while she proceeded to slowly pump what seemed like the contents of a decent sized lake through the catheters and into his bladder.

"Tell me when you can't take any more," she said after about two minutes pumping.

"I can't take any more," Blond gasped, almost before she'd got the words out of her mouth.

Then, while Blond was still standing there still holding his smock round his waist, trying desperately to pretend he was somewhere else, the nurse methodically consulted a graph on the machine which had been monitoring what had been going on in his bladder while she had been pumping it full of water. After making copious notes for what seemed to Blond longer than it took Tolstoy to write War and Peace she pointed to a plastic bucket. "Empty your bladder in there now," she ordered. Then getting to her feet she added primly: "I'll go outside while you do it to save your embarrassment."

As she made her way to the door Blond called after her. "Nurse!"

She turned. "Yes?"

"Nurse," Blond said, with great patience, "I have just lain down on an operating table while you have inserted two plastic tubes down my penis. I then had to stand up, still exposing everything I've got, while you pumped God knows how much water into my bladder. How could I possibly be any more embarrassed than I already am?"

The nurse smiled sweetly and went out.

Blond peed in the bucket. As he did so a problem other than his prostate trouble, a problem never far from his thoughts, the matter of his not having had sex for eight months, chose that moment, for no other reason than that you have to think about something while you're peeing in a bucket, to come back and haunt him. Granted almost six of those eight months had been spent in a coma, but that still left ten weeks, far too long a spell for a man of Blond's sexual appetite to go unsatisfied.

He eventually finished emptying his bladder. Almost immediately there was a tap on the door, as though the nurse had been listening out for the cessation of his flow.

"Come in."

The nurse entered. "All finished?"

"Thank God."

She quickly unhooked Blond from the equipment and withdrew the catheters from his penis, which proved to be a lot less painful than when she inserted them, Blond found to his great relief. "That's better," she smiled. Now that the unpleasant procedure was over she apparently no longer had to present the stern, no-nonsense attitude she found it prudent to employ when carrying out bladder examinations on male patients.

Blond looked at her and wished she had been more attractive. If she had been he would have….have what? He wouldn't have done anything, he ruefully admitted to himself. For during the past month he'd met half a dozen prospective conquests and hadn't propositioned a single one of them. The truth was that he was afraid they might rebuff him. He was of course fully aware that if a girl did turn him down it would in all probability be because she was having her period, but that didn't sweeten the pill any, didn't make him feel any better about it. So he just didn't proposition them anymore. And as a result had remained celibate.

The nurse was almost pretty when she smiled, Blond now noticed. But she was fat. So definitely not for him. But even if she had been attractive Blond knew in his bones that it was almost certain she would be having her period, so what would be the point? He breathed a deep sigh. It was hopeless. A Catch 22 situation.

"That's a very deep sigh, Mr Blond," the nurse said.

Blond looked at her. She really wasn't all that bad when she smiled. And she wasn't all *that* fat. Besides, he could always close his eyes and imagine she was someone with a more shapely figure. He came to a decision. Sod it, he said to himself, and taking the bull by the horns said to the nurse: "You're a very beautiful woman, Nurse. Would you like to make love with me?"

"I don't mind if I do," smiled the nurse.

They made love there and then, on the operating table. It was quite wonderful, every bit as good as it had been with any of the beautiful girls with stunning figures that Blond had bedded in the past. He thought he might try a plain girl next.

EPILOGUE

A little over a year later Blond was standing at the urinal in the gents toilets in the Grey Mare Inn. Since his last visit to Stockport his troublesome prostate gland had ceased to be a problem, the simple operation having restored his waterworks to A1 condition. Had he known the procedure was going to be as easy and stress free as it turned out to be he would have had it done long ago and saved himself much embarrassment.

Blond had been attending a small arms seminar in Manchester and at its conclusion had decided to stay overnight instead of returning immediately to London. Rather than remain in Manchester he had chosen to stay in Stockport, just six miles to the south east of the north's leading city.

James Blond was not a sentimental man - his profession didn't allow it - but during his short time in Stockport twelve months previously he had developed a sort of affection, if not for the town, then for its people, and his plan was to look one or two of them up. He had started at the Grey Mare Inn, and after a couple of pints with the landlord and the locals it was his intention to call in on Mrs Snockers and her lovely daughter Gloria. A get together with Divine Bottom was not out of the question.

It is in the nature of man, when standing at a urinal, to gaze up at the wall in front of him. Occasionally there is a window set in the wall through which he can look, but to do this is seldom rewarding as it is invariably glazed with frosted glass, rendering the view outside hazy if not entirely non-existent. He might just as well look at the wall. However the wall invariably offers a no more rewarding aspect, being tiled, as it is in the better establishments, or simply painted or whitewashed in the more humble conveniences. The man looks at it nevertheless.

What the man expects to see on the wall no one can say with any certainty. An amusing example of graffiti perhaps? Possibly, although men were in the habit of looking at the wall whilst urinating long before someone first had the idea of informing the world that Kilroy had once visited the premises, or that the contraceptive machine on the wall was a home for old semen.

One might be led to think, in view of what he was doing at the time, that it might be advantageous to look down, but urinating is a comparatively simple matter and a man would have to be especially dim-witted or a member of the aristocracy in order to piss on his shoes.

Some say it is an attempt to find a distraction, urinating being a boring business at the best of times. Or perhaps hopes are entertained of seeing a pair of flies copulating; anything being more interesting than urinating.

A few men eschew the wall above and the chances of seeing a bit of fly fucking and take their entertainment in directing their flow of urine at the disinfectant block nestling in the bottom of the urinal - an obvious target for the sporty, but not a rewarding experience for the majority of men as most of the entertainment value is nullified by the acrid smell of disinfectant mixed with urine that very soon begins to emanate from below.

Therefore the majority of men end up looking at the wall above the urinal. James Blond was no different in this respect. Which is why he was now looking at the wall above the urinal in the gents toilet at the Grey Mare Inn. When he had looked at the wall on his previous visit a year ago there had been nothing to see, save for a spider's web in the corner, the spider parked nearby anxiously awaiting its lunch. Since then however somebody, probably the landlord, had secured a small blue plaque to the wall. The inscription on it read: 'James Bond Peed Here'.

If you enjoyed reading James Blond – Stockport Is Too Much could you do me a couple of favours?

1. Review it on the Amazon Customer Reviews facility.

2. If you are a member of facebook, recommend it to your facebook friends. The very best way you can do this is to -

Type James Blond – Stockport Is Too Much in your facebook search box. Click on the James Blond book cover. This will take you to the James Blond page.

Tick the 'Like' box by the book's title.

Click on 'Suggest to friends' immediately below the book cover.

Select the friends to whom you wish to recommend the book to.

In the 'Add a personal message' box say what you think about the book. Tell them they can learn a little about it and read a sample chapter by logging on to http://www.facebook.com/pages/James-Blond-Stockport-Is-Too-Much/149469251769676

Click 'Send Invitations'.

Thanks for this

Terry Ravenscroft.

Also by Terry Ravenscroft and available on Amazon

Inflatable Hugh

"There seems to have been a long gap between the date of my brother's death and his funeral," observed Pugh.

"There was a rather unusual burial request," explained Oldknow. "He wanted to be buried in a vagina."

"In Virginia?" Pugh raised his eyebrows. "What's so unusual about that?" He knew that Aneurin had connections in the southern states of America, and whilst he could see why it might be a bit awkward, not to say inconvenient, burying someone in America who had met his end in Ramsbottom, Lancashire, he could see nothing particularly unusual about it.

The solicitor leaned back in his seat slightly and peered at Pugh over his spectacles. "Not Virginia, Mr Pugh. A vagina."

Pugh wasn't sure he'd heard correctly. "My brother wanted to be buried in a woman's minge?"

Oldknow winced at the crude language of the former Minister for Culture. "I'm afraid so. Not a real one of course. A coffin designed to look like one."

"Why on earth would he want to do that?"

"From what I've been told – although I didn't delve too deeply into it I must admit - he believed very much in the rejuvenating powers of the vagina."

"Rejuvenating powers?" Pugh was surprised to say the least. "He's not expecting it to bring him back to life, is he?"

203

Also by Terry Ravenscroft and available on Amazon

FOOTBALL CRAZY

Superintendent Screwer fixed Sergeant Hawks with a beady eye. When would they ever learn? "Where there is football, Sergeant, there is football hooliganism. Having been previously stationed at Leeds I know that for a fact; and I know all about the cancer in our society that football hooliganism has become."

"With respect sir, what few supporters the Town still have are nothing like Leeds United supporters."

Screwer glared at him. If Hawks had been the office door the paint would have blistered. "Respect?" he screamed. "Respect, Sergeant Hawks? You aren't showing me any frigging respect! If you were you wouldn't be arguing with me, you would be making plans to adequately police Frogley Town's opening game of the season!"

Hawks bit his lip. Retirement and that cottage in the Lakes suddenly seemed much farther away. "Yes sir."

Screwer drew in his horns a little. "Football supporters are the same the world over, Sergeant. Animals. Nothing more, nothing less. Take my word for it, just because the fans of Frogley Town have yet to reveal their true colours doesn't mean to say that one day they aren't going to."

"No sir."

The horns shot back out again as if spring-loaded. "Well just let them! They will not find the Frogley Police Force wanting. Not while my name is Herman Screwer they won't. We'll be ready for them, Sergeant. Ready to whip then into line; ready to break them; ready to smash the brainless bastards into submission!" He suddenly smashed his right fist into his left hand. The splat of the bone of his knuckles colliding with the flesh of his palm made Hawks wince. "Crowd control, that's the name of the game. What are we like for tear gas?"

CAPTAIN'S DAY

The problems posed by having a transvestite on the course were as nothing however once Philip had gone through the operation that transformed him into, if not a whole woman, then minus a set of male genitalia a whole woman. For it was then that Philip Hill, now Phyllis Hill, sought to play in the ladies' competitions, rather than the men's. Not surprisingly the Sunnymere ladies' section would not even contemplate the proposition. As far as they were concerned Phyllis Hill was still very much a man. That he was a man now minus a penis and testicles, in addition to being the proud owner, thanks to hormone treatment, of a pair of small but blossoming breasts, didn't even enter into the argument. The way the ladies saw it was that although Philip Hill may very well no longer have male genitalia he certainly still had the same muscular six feet two inch frame that he'd had before, as well as the two strong arms of the plasterer's mate he had been (and still was) for the last fifteen years, and therefore had an unfair advantage when it came to propelling a golf ball round the course, especially off the ladies' tees.

In an effort to reach some sort of compromise Phyllis had offered to play in the ladies' competitions but off the men's tees, but to no avail. The ladies would not allow her to play in their competitions full stop, and that was the end of the matter. The club chairman George Grover had pointed out to the ladies' committee, as delicately as he could, that Phyllis now had a vagina and bigger breasts than his wife, in fact bigger breasts than quite a number of the lady members, but the ladies had been adamant in their rejection of the new member without a member.

AIR MAIL

Air UK Ltd
Stansted House
Stansted Airport
Essex

Dear Air UK

I recently travelled with your airline, and what an exciting experience it was! It was the very first time that I have ever flown, but you can rest assured I will be flying with Air UK on many more occasions in the future if my first experience was anything to go by. Everything about the flight was excellent - although I have heard that Air 2000 could give you a run for your money as far as the in-flight catering goes - but what excited me the most was the sight of your stewardesses. How lovely they looked in their smart Air UK uniforms! And this gets me to the point of my letter. Is it possible to buy an Air UK stewardess uniform? I'm sure that if my wife owned one and she wore it at the appropriate time it would be all that was needed to but a bit of spice back into our sex life.

I look forward eagerly to your reply.

Yours sincerely

T Ravenscroft (Mr)

Air UK's reply follows

DEAR CUSTOMER SERVICES

The Jacob's Bakery Ltd
P.O.Box 1
Long Lane
Liverpool

Dear Jacob's Bakery

I am writing to you in my official capacity as secretary of the New Mills Invalids Club. This year marks the 25th anniversary of the club, and we mean to celebrate the occasion in some style, whilst at the same time giving club funds a much needed boost. To achieve this we intend to manufacture and sell to the general public a chocolate biscuit. We are confident that we have the expertise to accomplish this as four of our members used to work for the local sweet and confectionery factory - in fact it was because they worked at the local sweet and confectionery factory that they became invalids, having caught various parts of their anatomy in the machinery, but that's another matter.

Here is where you come in. I have long been a fan of your Jacob's Club biscuits, as have many of my fellow members, and to this end we would like to 'cash in' on your esteemed name by calling our biscuit a 'Jacob's Club Foot' biscuit. This would at once inform the public that it is a quality product, and also that it supports invalids. Can I have you permission, please?

Yours sincerely

T Ravenscroft (Mr)

Jacob's reply follows